GOSPEL STORIES

For Pastors, Teachers and Parents

ORVAL MOREN

"Happy are those who are strong in the Lord." Ps. 84:5

Orval Moren

ACW Press
Ozark, AL 36360

Gospel Stories
Copyright ©2005 Orval Kenneth Moren
All rights reserved

Cover Design by Alpha Advertising
Interior design by Pine Hill Graphics

Packaged by ACW Press
1200 HWY 231 South #273
Ozark, AL 36360
www.acwpress.com
The views expressed or implied in this work do not necessarily reflect those of ACW Press. Ultimate design, content, and editorial accuracy of this work is the responsibility of the author(s).

Publisher's Cataloging-in-Publication Data
(Provided by Cassidy Cataloguing Services, Inc.)

Moren, Orval Kenneth.

 Gospel stories : for pastors, teachers and parents / Orval Moren. --
 1st ed. -- Ozark, AL : ACW Press, 2005.

  p. ; cm.

  Includes bibliographical references and index
  ISBN: 1-932124-43-8

  1. Bible. N.T. Gospels--Homiletical use. 2. Bible--Homiletical use. 3. Bible stories, English. 4. Story sermons. 5. Meditations.
  I. Title.

BS534.5 .M67 2005
251--dc22   0502

Printed in the United States of America.

Dedication

To the Faith Lutheran Church members and families who listened to most of these children's sermons, and to my lovely wife, Bernell, who helped me with the visual aids, I dedicate this book. I thank her for her encouragement, and the congregation for their love.

Contents

Introduction

These stories are intended to be a resource for pastors, teachers and parents. You, as the storyteller might consider the story as a help and springboard for your own story. Although the stories may be read to the children just as written, I suggest the story is better when you tell it to them yourself.

I told the story first and then wrote it for you. If the story seems choppy and the sentences short, that's the way I told the story, and it's also the way the stories are written. Conversationally!

The bases for the story are the Bible readings, and the focus is on one possible single point of the Scripture. I know it is not easy to find a single point in some of the Bible readings, but remember you are telling the story to let the kids get *one* idea from the Scripture about Jesus and His people.

Whatever the setting, children come for the fun of hearing the story. They get an impression and a feel for the happening between Jesus and the people who listened to Him. By using a visual aid, the children will associate the point of the Gospel and the Lesson intended. That's enough! When the connection happens, your children's sermon, or children's story, or kids' time, has gone well!

All the Bible verses used are given in the index, with the biblical index as the primary organizing factor. The arrangements of Bible references begin with the pre-Christmas readings called Advent and end with the reading after Easter called Pentecost. As you look through the helps, you will discover many ways this book can help you as a resource.

Lesson:
Get Ready for Jesus

1 Advent (A)

Object: Play Shirt   Matthew 24:37-44

*M*ost of us are thinking about Christmas already! The stores are getting ready for the holidays and radios are playing Christmas music. But Christmas is not here yet. Rather, the time before Christmas is called Advent.

The message for Advent is "get ready for the coming of Jesus." We are preparing for Jesus' coming. He tells us in our Bible reading that no one knows for certain the hour or the day when the Lord shall come again. Only the Father in heaven knows!

So, Advent is the time for us to think about getting ready for Jesus. How do we get ready to meet Jesus? How would you answer that question? Would you say, "Go and hide"? No, that would not be good.

One way would be to play with our friends. Advent should be a time to have fun with friends. Why not! Let's play and have fun until Jesus comes. Jesus wants us to have fun. He wants us to be good and kind, and to enjoy all that we are and what we do. This play shirt can remind us to have fun!

Of course, we are also to be serious about Jesus. When we come to worship, we are quiet and we sing and pray. We are to set our minds on the Lord. All of us should be ready and waiting for Jesus and His church. But to hide would be a foolish way to prepare.

The Bible tells us that when we live in trust, love and grace, we are ready at play and work. Whatever we do—in school, in our home, at work or play—when we live for Him, share our faith, witness His love, we are ready. So, let us be ready by thinking on the Lord.

Lesson:
We Are Different. It Is Okay. 2 Advent (A)

Object: Bowl - small, of mixed fruit Matthew 3:1-12

How many of you like fruit? I want you to see my fruit bowl (or basket).

Here is an apple, a banana, and an orange. What else do we have? A pear, and grapes, too.

I have a question. Do you know that each fruit comes from a different tree? Apple and orange trees are each quite different. From one comes a fruit that is red and from the other a fruit that is orange. We need different kinds of trees for different kinds of fruit. Aren't you glad we have many kinds? Wouldn't you get tired of oranges only? Oh, you don't like oranges anyway! They make you sick! Well, that's too bad. But, we do need many kinds of fruit to have a variety for taste and diet.

You and I are different. Oh, yes, we are alike, too. Look around at the others here. What do you notice about us? Some of you are boys and some are girls. But even there, we are alike. For example, we all have two arms, two legs, two eyes, and two ears, along with one nose, one mouth and thirty-two teeth (if we have all of them). Yet, we are different. We have different color eyes, hair and skin. Trees, too, are different. All trees have leaves, branches and trunks, but all are different. Apples grow on apple trees but peaches do not grow on apple trees. It's just like you. Some of you can do some things very well, like music, art, math, spelling or computers.

In our Bible story, we read about a man who was very different. His name was John the Baptist. He didn't do things the usual way, but he did his best. God wants us to do our best.

The point is, it is okay to be different in our lives. However, the Lord wants our lives to show love, peace and happiness to others.

Lesson:
Be a Great Family

Object: Family tree and Branches   Matthew 11:2-11

I have a question for you. Do you know where you were born? Where were your mother and father born? Your grandparents? A different city or state? Or even another country? One of the best ways is to ask and put such information on a large piece of paper.

I have the places and names of my family on a poster. It looks like a tree. Some family trees are funny looking, like they are falling over on one side or fully wrapped together. Each family is different, just like trees are different.

At the bottom is just one family, and then it spreads out to my parents, my mother and dad. My mother had a mother and dad, my father also had a mother and dad. Everybody has a father and mother. We all have family trees of some kind. Some are so full they might tip over. On others, the branches are totally intertwined like a wild grapevine. Sometimes there are so many people related to us that we don't know them all. Many relatives can be like a puzzle.

It is good to have lots of people in the family. God wants us to be a great family. A great family does great things, things to be proud of, things that bring praise to the Lord. The church is God's family and they are the greatest. They are great because they do great things in the name of the Lord. They help people. They share love and joy. They comfort anyone who hurts and needs help.

A man named John the Baptizer was a great preacher. He wanted everyone to know God and be part of God's family. Aren't you glad you're a part of the Lord's family? Say with me, "I am part of the family of God, and, I am happy!"

Learn to Handle Fear

Object: Certificate/Bravery

Have you ever been afraid? Some people are always afraid. They have lots to fear. Everyone has some fear. I have been very afraid sometimes. Some fear is good because fear can protect us from danger. Policemen and firefighters often have fear.

Many men and women have jobs that are fearful. When they have been very brave, even in fear, we might present them with a "Certificate of Bravery" like this one. Maybe they saved someone's life, or stopped to help a family with a problem. Why do some people do brave things and others just pass by? Perhaps it's because they're afraid? Who knows! But we always want to thank those who are brave.

God once asked a young man to be very brave. He was in love with a young sweet girl. He wanted to marry her, and he planned to. But then he found out she was going to have a baby and he was not the father. He was very afraid and did not know what to do.

God sent an angel to the man in a dream, saying, "Don't be afraid." "Take this young girl named Mary to be your wife, because it will all work out just fine." Joseph was brave. He should have gotten a certificate like this to hang on the wall of his house in Nazareth. He did what the Lord's angel, Gabriel, asked. Joseph and Mary did get married. The angel told them the baby would be a boy, and they should name Him Jesus!

When you are afraid, remember the story about Joseph and Mary and baby Jesus! Learn to handle fear. Be strong for God. Let love replace fear in your life.

Lesson:

Jesus Was Born a Baby

Christmas (A)

Object: Baby Doll

Luke 2:1-20

*A*re you excited that it is Christmas? We know that nearly everyone celebrates Christmas as a holiday. Who can tell us what we celebrate? Yes! The birth of Jesus. Christmas is a birthday party for Jesus. We don't want to celebrate the "day" as much as we celebrate the birth of the Lord Jesus.

Jesus was promised long ago. Many prophets in the Old Testament had said that a messiah—a Savior—would come and bring peace and goodwill to all people. But no one was really sure how this Savior of the world would come. No one knew He would come as an infant. That was a total surprise. And no one knew the Lord would come so silently. We do kind of wonder about all the heavenly host who joined the angel. That must have been a large, beautiful chorus. We copy them. We sing songs of His birth like "Away in a Manger."

We also give gifts, like the wise men who came with gifts to honor the king.

We celebrate Jesus' birthday. But I want you to think about the baby Jesus himself. He was born. How big was He? We don't know for sure, but maybe the size of an average baby. How big is a baby? Oh, yes—very small.

Look at this doll. Baby Jesus was small just the way a doll is small. Babies need to be cared for. They need food, a diaper change, someone to sing and pray with them and to rock them. They need sleep, and more food and more sleep. Jesus was a baby.

But even at His birth Jesus was Lord. A baby, yes! Yet also, Lord from the beginning. When you play with your doll, or see someone play with a doll, remember baby Jesus! Jesus is the reason we have Christmas.

Lesson:
Moving Is Difficult

Object: Brochure/describing a city/town   Matthew 2:13-15, 19-23

Do you like surprises? Sometimes we get surprises we don't like very much. Let's pretend that your dad comes home from a long trip and brings a little book with pictures. Of course you are excited. Why did he bring this booklet home?

He opens the folder and says, "Surprise! I want everyone to have a good look, because we are moving to this place. It is a great place, and we will be there in a month or so." What a surprise! You are not sure you like this surprise.

You have many friends you have played together with many times. You had great fun. Now your dad comes home with the news that you are moving someplace else.

Sometimes we don't have much time to get ready to move. It is never easy to leave good friends and family, too. Can you remember moving? Tell me about it. How did you feel? You might feel bad, like you wanted to vote on it—or not go at all!

In our Gospel story Mary and Joseph, with baby Jesus, had to move in a very big hurry. They went a long way around to get home. But they did what had to be done. It was difficult. It was a crisis time. No questions asked. Move! Go!

When they got to the place they were supposed to be, they moved again, a second time. It was a dangerous time for baby Jesus and His family. When you read this Bible story about baby Jesus and His family, think how you would feel if you had to move today!

You might tell your mother and father how difficult it might be for you to move.

We Are Children of God

2 Christmas (A)

Object: Picture of a family

John 1:1-18

L et us look at a beautiful picture together. It is a picture of a family. How do we know they are a family? Yes, they are close. They smile. They seem to like each other. They are together. They look alike. Those are all good answers. Yes, they seem to be enjoying each other.

The woman is the girl's mother. Suppose they did not know each other. Would they look at each other? No! We usually don't relax much with strangers, do we? Rather, we are on guard. We are not sure we can trust strangers. It is always good to be very careful around strangers. Strangers are not friends at first. Later, they might be nice friends, but now they are strangers to us because we do not recognize their face. Friends are people we know, and who have received and given trust. Friends are people we believe and respect.

Trust is very important for all of us. Our Gospel reading today is about Jesus as the Word of Life and the people of God. The writer says that everyone who received Jesus received the right to be one of God's children. Children are small people who need tender loving care all the time. Children are not adults, they are only learning to be grown-ups and learning what is important for being an adult.

Children trust a lot. I trust. Do you trust? Trust means to depend on someone. Trust means honesty. Trust means that we expect our mothers and dads to keep their promises to us. To provide for us. To let us be children.

In this picture, we see a family who trusts each other, because they are children of God. Listen carefully to hear the word from the Gospel story. God's Word says, "To all who...believed in his name, he gave the power to become children of God." We are children of God. Wow! That's great!

Lesson:
Meaning of Baptism
1 Epiphany (A)

Object: Candle for baptism   **Matthew 3:13-17**

Yesterday was the twelfth day of Christmas, a day called Epiphany Day. Epiphany was the day the wise men might have come to find baby Jesus. They were looking for someone who would someday be the king of the Jews and king of the world. The world for them was not big, but it seemed awfully big.

Today is the first Sunday after the Epiphany. It's called the Baptism of our Lord Sunday. Jesus came to be baptized by John the Baptizer in the River Jordan. It was a very significant time in His life.

When children are baptized, they often receive a candle. We want everyone to know that Jesus is the light of the world and we are to be His light. Jesus Himself said that we were to be like a light, and we should let our light shine so that everyone could see it.

The candlelight reminds us that we have been baptized. We have been presented to the Lord for dedication and commitment. We have been prayed for. We have been blessed in baptism. God said, "You are mine." You could use a candle like this for a birthday party to remind yourself that Jesus is the light of the world to everyone who believes on Him.

The candle also means something else. See that little bird which looks like a dove on the candle. It tells us that Jesus was baptized. The voice came from heaven saying, "You are my beloved son, and I am well pleased with you." Baptism is God's work in us. He claims us as His children and makes us part of His family. Our part is to obey Him, do His will and be His children. Say with me, "I am a child of God. I will shine for Jesus."

Lesson:
We Are Lambs

2 Epiphany (A)

Object: Picture of a lamb

John 1:29-41

You all know what a sheep is, don't you? How many of you have seen one? Maybe you've seen them at the fair or at somebody's farm. Do you know that a lamb is a little sheep? I have a picture of a lamb. I want to tell you about this little lamb because this is a very important day and a very important story. It leads up to the beginning of Jesus' ministry. Jesus would have the power and authority of God.

One day Jesus came to one of His friends. His name was John. John had said, "Jesus baptized with the Holy Spirit."

There were people who were saying that Jesus was the Lamb of God. John also said as he saw Jesus, "This is the Lamb of God."

Those people really knew what the phrase "Lamb of God" meant, because it was talked about in the Hebrew Scripture which we call the Old Testament. A prophet there named Isaiah had said this would happen (Isaiah 53).

The next day, Jesus came again to where John was, and John said again, "Behold the Lamb of God."

The people got very excited. They thought, "We are going to follow Him, because here is a man who is kind and gentle. This man comes from God. He is the 'Lamb,' and someday He will be our shepherd."

We have come here today to worship and give our praise to Jesus, who is the Lamb of God. What John wants us to know is this: We are like little lambs and Jesus is now the shepherd of the flock. We are to follow the shepherd. We ask the Lord Jesus to lead and guide our lives as we grow older, so that all a shepherd promises to the sheep is ours.

Lesson:
Win—"Catch"—People To Christ

Object: Short fishing pole/red-heart hook   Matthew 4:12-23

I have a fishing pole. It has a special hook. What does the hook look like? A red heart. Here is the story: Jesus did not work alone. He had many people with Him. Some were especially chosen and were called disciples. In our Gospel today Jesus said the disciples would catch men. He would teach them to make followers and believers. We are followers! We believe Jesus!

Jesus called to a man named Andrew. Andrew went and got his brother Simon called Peter. Then two more brothers came along named James and John. How many is that? Four. How many disciples did Jesus call all together? Twelve. Yes! That is all ten fingers, plus two!

Let us look at this fishing pole with a heart for a hook. This pole and the cross on the heart tell us a message. We are to bring the good news that Jesus wants us to be followers of Him. We are to be His people.

Jesus wants you to be a fisher of men and women and children. We are His people. We are baptized and we believe Jesus is our Lord and Savior. This fishing pole tells something about us as Christians. The heart with the cross tells us to draw people in as a fisherman catches fish.

I was a little boy about nine years old when I felt that Jesus wanted me to be like an "Andrew." It took many years of thinking and praying and wondering before I became a pastor. Finally, I understood that Jesus calls to us to share our lives and His good news with others. We are to fish, with a pole and a hook like this. Be like an Andrew. Jesus was happy for him. He asks all of us to fish for Him. Isn't that wonderful? We have a great responsibility even when we are very young like you are.

18

Lesson:
The Kingdom and Righteousness   4 Epiphany (A)

Object: Cook's paper hat   Matthew 5:1-11

I have something different for us today. It's this object. A piece of paper with a blue stripe on it. Who thinks they know what it is? It's a cooking hat, a hat that looks like an army cap. Where do we use these in the church? In the kitchen. We want our food to be clean, and we want to look clean as the food is prepared and served. Eating is one of the most important things we do in life. This hat tells us about our kitchen, our food, our lives and being clean.

In the Gospel, Jesus is telling us something very interesting. It has to do with a hat like this. If you are wearing a hat, you know that you are going to get good food for your body. The food is fresh. It is well prepared and tasty. We want the food we eat to make us strong and healthy. But Jesus is saying something else goes along with that. It's what is on the inside of you, like your faith and kindness and gentleness and goodness. How you help one another and heal hurts. How you're good to one another and befriend one another.

Jesus uses a big word for all that God gives us. The word is righteousness. Let's say it together, shall we? Righteousness. Let's say it once more quite loud. RIGHTEOUSNESS. It comes from God. It tells what is on the inside of you that shows on the outside. It is not just a covering over to make you look nice. You are really nice on the inside *and* outside. It's very, very important because it tells us something about the kingdom of God. In the Gospel story, we read about a teaching from Jesus called the Sermon on the Mount. In that sermon, Jesus tells us how to be happy. What this means is, we live by grace, meaning God's favor, and not by law. So we are righteous and have the kingdom.

Lesson:
Let Us Shine

5 Epiphany (A)

Object: Basket/deep/to cover a candle   **Matthew 5:13-20**

Jesus told us He was the light of the world. In the Gospel reading we heard the word "light" again. The Scripture was part of the Sermon on the Mount. He is the light of the world, and He wants us to be His light bearers. Wherever we go, we are to be lights. We are not to hide our light or to put out our light. We are to let our light shine. How do we shine when we are small and young as you are? Well, there might be many ways. One of the ways we can show this is to lift up one of your fingers high and say, "I am a light." Do that with me.

I have this deep basket which is like a bowl. If we put it on top of the light, what happens? The light is covered. Remember what Jesus said? "Do not cover up your light with a basket or a bowl." Why not? Because the basket may catch on fire. Yes, that's right! But also, the light may go out. And, you are covering up your light. You need to let your light shine. The light is like your life. Don't cover up your life. Don't hide your faith, or be ashamed of it.

I want you to sing a song with me! First of all, pretend that your index finger is a light. Raise your hand and point your finger toward the sky. Hold your light high. Now sing with me:

Verse 1: This little light of mine, I'm going to let it shine. *(2 times)*
      Let it shine, let it shine, let it shine.

Verse 2: Hide it under a basket? NO! I'm going to let it shine. *(2 times)*
      Let it shine, let it shine, let it shine.

Verse 3: Shine all over (our city, church, etc.) I'm going to let it shine. *(2 times)*
      Let it shine, let it shine, let it shine.

That is a good song. We should let our light shine wherever we go: in school, at play, with our friends, in our homes. Everywhere. Let your light shine.

Lesson:
Control Your Anger

6 Epiphany (A)

Object: Jar of water

Matthew 5:20-37

What do I have here? It's a jar of water. I have a question for you. Where does water come from? The faucet? Sure it does. But where else does it come from? Inside the earth! How about lakes and rivers? How about the clouds in the sky? Clouds produce the rain, and the rain is water. But rain can also turn into something else before it hits the ground. What is that called? Snow. If it is cold, water can turn into ice. Ice is water that has been frozen.

Water and sunshine are very necessary. They are totally important for us to live and to grow. Water and sunshine come to all people. The Bible says they come to the just and the unjust, the good and the bad. The water from the rain and the sunshine are God's blessings upon us to help us.

As we grow up our bodies grow stronger. And our minds and our hearts and our spirits are to grow up in the Lord. The Gospel reading for today talks about the kinds of changes that happen to us as we grow. There might be anger in our lives. Jesus told us about anger. It is not good to have uncontrolled anger. Jesus talked about hurting or killing someone. That is the result of uncontrolled anger. He also talked about wanting everything for ourselves. That is wrong and a sin.

Sometimes when we get too angry, our mother or dad might put a little water on us to calm us down. It is amazing how water works. Water is good. When crowds of people get very angry, police and firefighters use water to calm them down so they can think again. Water can cool down people and things. Jesus loved water.

Make a New Beginning

Object: Coloring book and crayons   Matthew 5:38-48

I have a coloring book and some crayons. It is always fun to color, especially if you have a new book and new crayons. You all know there are three basic colors: red, yellow, and blue. It is important to learn how to color so your work is neat and nice. Follow the lines. Mix your colors well. Be creative. Think what you want to do. Once you have colored a page, you cannot undo it.

Do you know what happens sometimes? A child or young person doesn't like the looks of the page, so they tear it out in frustration. Jesus is not happy with uncontrolled anger and revenge. They crumple it up and throw it on the floor. Jesus is not happy with uncontrolled behavior. Instead when you color, the right thing is to leave that page and go on to a new one. Make a new beginning! Jesus teaches us instead to make a new beginning.

One time when Jesus was talking with a large group of people, He said, "Love your enemies! Pray for those who persecute you!" (Matthew 5:44, TLB). What that means is to pray for those who dislike you. Of course, Jesus was talking about love. Love is thinking good and kindness for someone who might not like you. Love is doing right for others. I think the Lord is pleased when we treat each other with love and forgiveness and gentleness.

When you color in your book, think of Jesus. He went to school, too, of course. There were no crayons or coloring books in those days. When things go wrong for you, make a new beginning. Jesus said control your anger and start over. He said love one another, even those who don't color very well, and be friends. Color nice!

Lesson:
God Will Provide for Our Needs   8 Epiphany (A)

Object: A check/blank check book   Matthew 6:24-34

The Gospel story today is one of the greatest promises ever made by Jesus. We need to have food to eat, and good water for drinking. We need sleep and shelter. God has promised all of these. But are they all free? Yes, because God makes it possible. But also, no, because we are expected to plan and work. The birds work hard. They are up early. They build nests. It takes a lot of work to build a nest. Have you ever watched a bird build one? A nest takes hundreds of trips. When there are babies in the nest, it is hard work for mama bird to find insects and worms for her young ones. But she doesn't need to worry.

So what about us? How do we get what we need? We all like money. I like money. Do you like money? We want everything we see. We think we need everything we want. We want candy suckers. We want ice cream. We want new toys. We want new things of all kinds. We have many wants.

How many of you know what I am holding? It is a check. Checks can be used to get money from a bank. But this check is blank. How much is a blank check worth? Nothing? Something? Everything? It depends! Yes, it depends on the amount of money we have in the bank.

The Lord has given us a blank check for our life. We will get what we need, but not everything we want. That is Jesus' promise. He said, "Seek the Lord's kingdom first, and God will provide what you need." Do you get all the candy you want? Of course not. The promise is that God will help us just as He does the birds of the air and the flowers in the field or garden. God wants us to have a strong faith. He also wants us to be very smart about what we need.

Warmth of Jesus

Transfiguration (A)

Object: The Sun

Matthew 17:1-9

Today is a very special day. I want you to do something with me. I want you to pretend that the sun isn't shining. Close your eyes. Everybody close their eyes. Put your hands over your eyes. No peeking! Pretend that we know the sun isn't shining. We do not know when to get up because it's still dark. It's night. If we get up, we walk in the dark because there is no light anyplace, and outside it's dark. The plants cannot grow because they don't have any sunlight. The birds don't know when to wake up, because it's dark. Keep your eyes closed. Since there is no sunlight, it's getting very cold. Everybody shiver a little bit. Let your bodies feel cold. It's cold out there.

Open your eyes, but remember, the sun isn't shining. Think about the darkness and the light. Remember this: The light is a reminder to us of God's presence. The sun is like God's love. It's warm, and keeps us cozy and warm. We know that God loves us. When the sun doesn't shine, things die. We get cold and we are freezing. You all know what it means to be cold.

The Gospel tells a story about Jesus on the mountainside with three disciples. The light shone very brightly. The hearts of the three with Jesus were warmed. From this story we learn that Jesus had come to earth from His home in heaven. The disciples were afraid. Jesus came and touched them. Touching is comforting. It is amazing how often and how many people He touched. From this story, we get an idea of what it is like for Jesus to be with God. We know what it is like when the warmth of the sun is upon us. Today is a special day we call Transfiguration. It is the time Jesus got a glimpse again of His heavenly home.

Lesson:
Sin Tempts Us

1 Lent (A)

Object: Key/room or house   Matthew 4:1-11

The first Sunday in Lent begins today. There is something different about the worship service. We have different kinds of hymns and different choir songs. Our worship is more somber, which means gloomy. The first Sunday in Lent is different than Christmas and Epiphany, which are happy days.

I have a room key as an object lesson. I want you to pretend with me that we are in one little room, all of us. I want you to bunch up close to me. Come on in! Get close! Here's what we are going to do. Everybody is in the room and the door is shut. I am going to lock it. Turn the key.

Now, that is what we are like—squashed. We are in a room, and we can hardly move in here. We can't have any fun because we're all squeezed together. We have no freedom. We can't run. We can't play. In fact, we can hardly breathe because it is so warm and stuffy. Maybe we are wondering if we will ever get out. Who has the key? Where is the room key? Pretend we cannot find it. It got lost under the rug by the door. Now, sit back and listen, because something like this happened to Jesus.

In our Gospel story, Jesus is tempted by the devil. The devil wanted to lock up Jesus and throw away the key. He wanted to squeeze Jesus into a scary place.

It feels good, warm and cozy to be close together. But when you are locked in, then the feeling gets scary. The devil wanted Jesus to feel good. The devil would have boxed Him in, then Jesus would have lost sight of His mission. That would be sin. The devil tempts us, too. He wants us to forget about God. Our key reminds us that we can unlock the door.

Jesus Refreshes Us 2 Lent (A)

Object: Glass of water John 4:5-26

When were you really thirsty? Remember that time? What was the best drink you could think of to quench your thirst? Milk, pop, juice, or what?

Here is a glass of cool water. Doesn't it look refreshing? How many of you could use a drink right now?! Water is very necessary for life. Everyone needs water every day.

The Gospel tell us a story of a woman who came to a very old well to draw out water. It was called Jacob's well, because he had dug it. It was very deep and large. The water was cool and good. Remember, in those days there was no running water, no water from a fountain or faucet as we have. Everyone had to carry water. The well was a gathering place for the children and their mothers. Everybody had to draw water. They would let down a bucket and pull it up with a rope or on a lifting drum.

The woman was thirsty and needed water for her home. Jesus came to the well and offered her not only water, but living water as well. He said He had the water of life. What it meant was that Jesus has the best for us in life. Jesus came to give all of us what He called "living water."

He told he woman, "It was the gift of God" to drink such water. Naturally, the woman got excited. Not only that, Jesus told her everything she had done. Some of those things were not so nice. She really got excited that He knew about her life. But then Jesus said, "The water that I give will become a spring of living water, welling up to eternal life." Somehow she got the message that Jesus wants the best for us. Jesus brings us God's promise, which gives us the water that satisfies, just like it did the woman at the well.

We Can See with Light   3 Lent (A)

Object: Film Slide/of yourself   **John 9:1-41**

How many of you know what this is? A slide. This is the frame, and on the inside? A picture. What do we need to have if we are going to see what is in the picture? We need the sun to shine through. What machine do we need? We need a film projector, so we can have light. So, we put the slide into the projector and we can see it. But we can also hold it up to the sun.

We are something like this slide. We need light so people can see how beautiful and bright we are. That is what Jesus has done in our lives. He makes us beautiful and bright so people can see who we are. We can see because there is light. If there is no light, it is all darkness. It is like when our eyes are closed and we cannot see anything. Everybody close their eyes. Can you see anything? Not a thing. It is as if we are blind. We can't see!

In the Gospel story there was a blind man who had never seen light. Jesus gave healing and sight to him. He was so happy. He told everyone!

People asked, "Who made you well?"

He said, "The man called Jesus."

"How did He do this miracle?"

The man blind from birth said, "I don't know, but I know I see!"

Some people got upset because Jesus told them they were blind in their hearts. That means they could see with their eyes, but they were blind to God. But we can see because there is light all around us, and in us, through Jesus. This light is something like our lives. Jesus wants us all to see Him. He is the light of the world, and He brings light into our hearts and lives.

Lesson:
Learn to Serve

Object: Wheelchair

A wheelchair is made so it can move with someone sitting in it. It is a great invention. Some chairs have electric motors. Some people are so strong they can power their chairs with their arms. If you were to push the chair for someone, you must be careful of cars, stairs and steps and stones.

The wheelchair becomes like a car, doesn't it? It's like a little scooter so someone can get around. Sometimes things go wrong. For instance, a foot can get out of place from where it was supposed to rest. Some things can also go wrong in a person's body. That's why people sit in wheelchairs. Something happened in an accident or they may have a health problem.

If you met somebody in a wheelchair, how could you help them? How about opening doors or climbing steps. They might need an elevator. Someone must serve and help. How about if they can't reach the fountain to get a drink of water? What would you do? You might have to find a glass so they could get a drink.

How could you help the most? You know the biggest thing of all? You need to help them to help themselves so they can become independent and do what they need to do when other people aren't around. That would be the most important thing you could do to help. Jesus said in the Gospel reading that we are to serve. When we serve, we want to serve for the right reasons. If we serve to get all the credit and glory, that would be bad. If we serve to get noticed and praised, we are really selfish. We should serve in unselfish love. That means we help other people in a way that they can help themselves to the best. We learn to serve.

Lesson:

Sad and Glad Feelings   5 Lent (A)

Object: Plate/paper, Face/happy one side - sad on other   John 11:1-53

I have a very smiley face. (Show the happy side of the face.) We smile when we are happy. Everybody smile with me. Good!

In our Gospel story today, which is a very, very long reading, Jesus came to His friend's house. The names of these people were Mary and Martha and their brother Lazarus. Jesus stayed at their house often. These friends lived in Bethany, which was about a two-hour walk from the capitol city of Jerusalem. Jesus would stop over for a place to stay and have dinner. Martha was a very good hostess, always buzzing around. Jesus was happy with these friends. But today was different.

Jesus and His friends looked like this (sad face). His friend Lazarus had died four days ago. The family had looked for Jesus and waited and waited for Him to come. Messengers had been sent, but no one knew where Jesus was. They looked everywhere. Finally, He came, four days after His friend died. Everyone was sad! Can we be sad, too? Everybody be sad! Jesus was so sad that He wept. That means He cried. It was a very sad time.

Being happy or sad are gifts from God. We call them feelings. They can change very fast. Let me show you. Watch the face (sad). Be sad! Now, be happy and glad. See the face (glad). Sad and glad are not far apart. They are very strong feelings! Jesus had feelings. He could cry. He could laugh. Here is a story where He cried. It is okay to cry. Sometimes we need to cry. When we cry, the Lord is with us to help us through sadness until we come to gladness again. We all have sad and glad feelings.

Lesson:
Honor the King

Object: Carpet/red piece   **Matthew 21:1-11**

In the days of Jesus, when somebody very important was coming to town, they would put nice clothing down on the road in front of the person being honored so he could walk on it. Or, he would ride on a donkey and come into town like a king would do. They would do what we call putting down the red carpet" (show the carpet) to honor the person.

What is this green branch? You all know what this is. It's a palm branch, isn't it? Sure, it's something that grows in the field and on the trees. They laid these branches down on the road like a carpet. This was a sign that a person was honored and respected. Palm branches then were like a red carpet now. People wanted to honor their leaders. They needed to show respect and loyalty. That's also why we have a red carpet or a parade. They knew something really wonderful and lots of fun was happening that day. Jesus came to town. He came into Jerusalem.

All the people said, "Hosanna!"

"Hosanna" is a strange word. It means to praise God. Actually, it means, "Lord, save us." They were excited and waiting, expecting a king to come. They thought Jesus was the king, and they were going to give Him honor and respect. They were going to give Him a huge parade for the Passover, because that was a really fun time in the life of Israel. They all said, "Hosanna." Everybody say it with me. "Hosanna." Once more! "Hosanna." We want to praise Jesus for all that He has done for us. We know that next Thursday is Holy Thursday with a special Lord's Supper, the Communion. On Friday it is Good Friday. Then comes Resurrection Sunday. Jesus gave His life for us. Say it again: Hosanna!

Lesson:
New Life

Object: Easter lily

I want you all to look at all the Easter lilies that have been provided for our church today. We want to talk about this beautiful flower called a lily.

Notice the beautiful green color of the plant. Green is the color we usually associate with growth. We think of trees that grow leaves and green flowers and green grass. We know that means growth. So, the green of this plant tells us something about new life. This beautiful flower reminds us that Jesus has risen from death into new life.

Easter is exciting because new life and hope comes through resurrection. Easter Sunday is very special for all of God's people. We are all here dressed in our very best clothes. We have come to this service of worship on Easter Sunday because Christ has risen.

I want you all to say that with me: "Christ has risen."

Once more. "Christ has risen."

Now, that's what these flowers are saying, as these white horns point in different directions. They are proclaiming to everybody that Christ has risen. Jesus died on the cross, then He was buried in a tomb. When some people came to the cemetery, they were surprised that Jesus was gone. Some were happy. Others were afraid. The good news is that Christ is alive. White is a good color. The beautiful white color tells us that there is purity. The white color announces there is beauty and that, indeed, Christ has risen from death. We praise the Lord for the power of the resurrection. The Easter lilies give us the lovely fragrance of the resurrection.

Lesson:
Jesus Rose from the Dead

2 Easter (A)

Object: Picture of a butterfly

John 20:19-31

Last Sunday we celebrated resurrection when Jesus rose from the dead. What is the main symbol for resurrection? How many of you had an Easter egg hunt? That's a good symbol, but that's not the best symbol for the resurrection. How about all the Easter lilies that were here last Sunday? The church was filled with these beautiful flowers. They gave a beautiful aroma all over the church. That is a better symbol of resurrection.

I've got a resurrection symbol in this box. Do you want to see what it is? Let me turn and tip the box. Listen! Do you think it's a heart? Do you think it might be words of love? What is it? A beautiful butterfly. That's the main symbol of the resurrection.

When you're out playing in your back yard or in a park or someplace where there are flowers, look for a butterfly. When you see these butterflies flitting around, remember they symbolize new life. Remember that Jesus had been put on the cross. On the third day after His death, He appeared to some followers and disciples. Jesus came to them saying, "Peace be with you," and also, "Receive the Holy Spirit." One of the disciples named Thomas was not there. But, later he was, and he believed that something special had happened to Jesus. All of them were afraid, but happy, too.

Maybe they acted like a butterfly. They're just out there flying around having fun. They couldn't even care less. But they symbolize new life and that is wonderful. The disciples were not sure what happened to Jesus, or what to do, but one thing for sure. They were sure Jesus rose from the dead. And so are we!

Lesson:
Lord's Supper and Jesus
3 **Easter (A)**

Object: Bread/small loaf or bun
Luke 24:13-35

In the Gospel story, Jesus met two men walking on the road to their home in the town of Emmaus. The men didn't know who was asking them questions about the past week. They talked about Jesus who had been betrayed, and all the nasty things that had happened on Passover. It had been a terrible week.

Passover was supposed to be a fun time. People came from everywhere for the party. They would walk for many miles to attend. Passover was a really big celebration, like a family reunion picnic and Fourth of July all put together into a Thanksgiving Day party. It celebrates the time the Jews were set free after many hard years in Egypt as slaves.

These two men had walked about seven miles from their village into Jerusalem for the Passover. But the weekend was bad, because there had been a lot of fighting and turmoil. Three men were crucified, put on a cross to die. One of them was Jesus. Now these two men were walking home, talking along the way. The stranger didn't seem to know what had gone on during the week.

When evening came, they invited this stranger who had walked with them into their home for supper. They still did not know who He was. But then as supper was prepared, Jesus did something, which gave them an instant clue as to who He was. What did He do? The resurrected Jesus took the bread (like this loaf) and broke it into several parts. On the night of His betrayal, Jesus had done exactly the same thing. He said that sharing the bread and the wine would help them remember Him. And now they knew! They realized Jesus was resurrected and present with them. When we come to the communion, you know we break bread to remember the Lord Jesus Christ.

Lesson:
Hear the Voice of Jesus and Follow   4 Easter (A)

Object: Tape recording, voices of pastor, & two others   John 10:1-10
   well-known voices (read from John 10:3-4)

When your parents ask you to come, or ask you to do something, how well do you hear and listen? Hearing is important, and listening is a great skill. In order to listen well, we need to hear first. We learn to hear and listen.

Sometimes a parent or teacher will say "listen." They want your attention. They want not only your ears to hear, but also your mind to think. Hearing and listening are not the same. Listening is more. If someone says, "It is time for work," we may not want to listen and obey. But if someone says, "Let's get ice cream," we hear right away. We call that "selective listening," meaning listening to what you want to hear.

I have some voices on this cassette player. I will play one. Hear and think, if you know whose voice it is. Who was that? You know the voice. Whose voice is it? (Pastor.) You heard and you listened to your pastor (or friend).

In the Gospel reading, Jesus said that sheep know the shepherd's voice. They will follow the voice. They are trained. They just naturally know what to do, just like us.

If the teacher says, "Line up and follow me," we know the voice and we know what to do. We are like sheep. We will follow the voice.

Jesus said He has the voice through the words that we are to hear. How does Jesus' voice come to us? We hear Jesus' voice through the stories in the Bible. We hear Him when we care for and love people. When someone speaks words of kindness and gentleness, of course, you will follow that soft and gentle voice. Learn to listen and follow and speak softly.

34

Lesson:
Be Able to Read the Gospel Map

Object: Map/road

One time Jesus told the disciples of a great promise. He said there were many rooms in God's heavenly home. The disciples were excited about such a home. But for some reason they also were very troubled and sad. Maybe it was because Jesus had told them He was leaving. They could not understand why He would want to leave them. The disciples were always hoping and waiting for Jesus to be the new king. They wanted Him to be like the governor or even the president. It would be right for a king to have a big house with many rooms. But why would Jesus lead them to think He was going away? They wanted Jesus to begin the planning for a new nation. They called it the "Kingdom." It means the domain of the king. When someone leaves, we are sad. Would you all agree? How do you feel when someone leaves and will not be back? Sad and sorrowful! Of course, that's how we all feel!

The disciple Thomas was especially upset about this word from Jesus. He wanted to visit the place where Jesus was going, since Jesus seemed to insist on going away. He said, "Where are you going? How can we know the way?" Jesus told him, "I am the way. You get to God's home through Me."

I have this road map. It is something like Jesus' answer. If we follow the map, reading it correctly, we should arrive at the place Jesus wants us to be. We can chart the roads, add the mileage, figure out the time, and arrive safely. The Bible is something like our map in the church. We want to know the Bible very well, so it can be the road map for us in our home and church. It is very important for us to study the map carefully. Know the map. Be able to read it. And finally, trust the map!

35

Lesson:
Keep the Commandments

Object: Heart/picture of love, or paper/wood plaque   John 14:15-21

How many of you have heard of the commandments? How many are there? Twelve! No, there are twelve disciples. Three! No, that is the Trinity: Father, Son and Holy Spirit. How many of you say "ten." Yes, there are ten commandments. Look at your hands and count fingers. Ten. There are ten commandments.

Jesus said, "If you love me, you will keep my commandments." Was He referring to His commandments, or the ten in the Old Testament? Or both? Let us say both! Jesus gave us two new commandments.

I have a heart of love to show to you. When we see a heart, we know it is not talking about the part of our body that goes "thump, thump." That is our heart muscle, which pumps blood through the arteries of our bodies. Rather, we are talking about all that we are. Everything that is you and me. This heart means that my whole being—mind and spirit and body—are doing what God wants. Jesus said, "We have the Father's love as we keep the commandments."

The Bible tells us to love the Lord our God with all our heart. All that we are! We have the power to do that perfectly through the Holy Spirit. It takes power to love and to keep the commandments. Love and commandments, power and the Holy Spirit are God's gifts to each of us.

In the Gospel story, Jesus called the Spirit the Counselor or the Helper. He will reveal the great truth about God. The great truth is that God is love. God loved the world and sent Jesus. Jesus turned the commandments into grace. Grace is God's gift of love. That is the great truth. When you keep the commandments as guidelines, you live by grace. Remember the heart of love.

Lesson:
Your Life Should Bloom   7 Easter (A)

Object: Flower/blooming plant   John 17:1-11

T his is a beautiful plant! (show it) Notice how healthy it looks. Look at the white flowers blooming and look at the dark green leaves. I wonder why it looks so nice. Why is it so healthy? Probably it is planted in good soil. It probably gets water and the right amount of sunshine and fresh air. Who knows all the things that go to make this pretty blooming plant!

As we look at this blooming flower, it reminds us that God wants all of us to bloom. That's right. All of us are beautiful people. Every one of us is a beautiful person. God wants us to bloom where we are. He wants us to have a strong faith and to have lots of love and kindness in our life. He wants us to share Jesus with other people and be helpful to our parents and friends. He wants you to bloom wherever you are.

How can you as a child bloom? You can smile. You can be nice. You can be pretty. Keep yourself clean and orderly. Have you noticed how orderly and nice plants are? They can be our example. Be a beautiful person, just the way God made you to be. Jesus wants you to be a lovely flower for Him.

In the Gospel reading, we have a long prayer from Jesus. It is not an easy prayer. It is hard to understand some of it. One part of the prayer is easy. He wants all of us to have eternal life. Such a life begins now, just like a beautiful flower such as this one. Jesus prayed that His disciples and everyone would know God and glorify God. He wanted them to bloom in their life and faith like this flower. Our lives are to have purpose and meaning. There are many kinds of flowers with many colors, many shapes and many nice smells. We are to bloom like a beautiful flower in someone's life and make them happy!

Lesson:
We Are the Church

Object: Seeds/beans/one white, one brown   John 20:19-23

I have two seeds in my hand. One is white and is called a pole bean, meaning it grows best on a trellis—on a frame that holds up the vines and leaves. The other is brown and is called a pinto bean. It grows best on the ground like a small bush plant. Each bean produces a very different type of bean. But both are called beans.

These beans are like you and me and the church. We are each different—different color, different size and different faces. But we are all a part of the church, the people of God, just like a bean is a bean even though it might be a different color or shape.

We are the church. We serve the Lord Jesus. We help people. We heal hurts in the name of Jesus. It does not make any difference about what color bean we are. God's people are living everywhere in the world. All have different color skin. Some are very brown, some tan, others are black and some are white. Some of God's people are old, some young, some smart, some poor, some do wonderful things.

Jesus came to His disciples saying, "Receive the Holy Spirit, and peace be with you." When the Holy Spirit lives in you, you are a link in the church. Jesus wants our lives to be powered by the Holy Spirit. The Holy Spirit makes the church grow, like soil makes the beans grow into plants that produce a large bean crop, some brown and some white, some on a trellis and some on the ground. But, do you know what? Beans are beans. And we are Christians of every kind. We love Jesus, and we want His blessing in our lives so that we can show His love to each other.

Lesson:
God Is One in Three   Trinity Sunday (A)

Object: Triangle/wood/paper   Matthew 28:16-20

On Trinity Sunday, we honor God as Father, Son and Holy Spirit. I have a triangle to show you. I want you to notice that it is like the trinity of God: three sides and all are equal. But each side also is a part of the other, one is Father, one Son and one is Holy Spirit. All look the same. Each is necessary. Each is important. We do not understand how God is One in Three. We simply know it.

Jesus spoke of all three parts. He told us to baptize in the name of God: the Father and Son and Holy Spirit. Whenever there is a baptism, either a baby or a child or an adult, we are always baptized into the name of God—Father, Son and Holy Spirit. Our Lord is one God, yet there are three parts: the Creator, the Redeemer and the Power.

In our Gospel reading, Jesus commands us to tell the good news that He had authority and power from God the Father. He wants us also to have power to tell. As God's people, we have power in the Spirit. We have power and authority to do God's will.

We have a promise, a purpose, a people and the Lord's presence with us. All of this is good news. Let this triangle remind you of God, who is our Father, and the Son and the Holy Spirit. It is called the symbol of the Trinity.

Jesus said, "Go everywhere…to all people and make them my disciples." We are commanded to "make" disciples. Think about this. Were you "made" a child of God? Sure you were. God has wanted to bless you so He put a claim on you and said, "You are my child." It begins with baptism, which is God's idea. We baptize in the name of God: Father, Son and Holy Spirit. We preach and teach in the name of God. The triangle teaches us a lesson.

Lesson:
We All Have Limited Time 1 Advent (B)

Object: Timer, egg or kitchen type Mark 13:33-37

I have a question for you. How many years would you like to live? Sixty. Seventy-eight. Ninety-one. Who knows of anyone over a hundred? A hundred years is a long time. Some people live longer than others. The Lord wants all of us to live as long as possible. To do that we must live healthy. We must be smart about living. Eat smart! Exercise regularly!

Who knows what a birthday means? A birthday means one year has come and gone for you. We can measure time by the day of our birth.

I have this timer. It counts minutes. It helps to keep time, just for a little while. Think about your life. (Set it.) Those clicks are like your life. The time goes by quickly. Ask your dad and mom about how quickly time goes. We are to use our time wisely, doing the Lord's will. We are all to have purpose and meaning in our lives.

God puts us in the world to have fun and to help each other and, most of all, to enjoy His wonderful creation. However, we know from the Gospel story that we are to watch and pray, because we do not know when the clicker will go off or when our time on earth is gone. So we are to be ready. Ready means to believe that Jesus will come—ready or not. Ready is to be prepared.

Jesus said it is like a man who went on a trip. As he left home, he hired someone to water and mow the grass, others to care for everything inside, and still others to watch because no one knew when the man would return from the trip. Everything was to be ready. Jesus told this story so we would be prepared and live for the Lord in all that we do.

Lesson:
Holy Spirit/Hot for Jesus

2 Advent (B)

Object: Flame/Advent Candle

Mark 1:1-8

On the second Sunday of Advent, we light the second candle. How many are left? Two! Two Sundays until Christmas.

You all know that candles have a flame that is hot, right? We can get burned from a candle, so we are always very careful with candles in church, and at home, too. It is fun to watch a candle flame flutter. Flutter means that the flame seems to move in and out.

The Bible compares the Holy Spirit to a flame of fire. It moves around within us, and warms our hearts.

In the New Testament there was a great preacher named John who baptized many people, including Jesus. He said Jesus would come to him to be baptized. John declared that Jesus would be even greater than he was, because Jesus would be baptized with the Holy Spirit. His words were, "After me is coming one who is stronger than I am, whose sandals, in all humility, I am not to stoop down and tie the laces. I have baptized you with water. He will baptize you with the power of the Holy Spirit." John was a strange man, yet a very powerful preacher.

Candlelight suggests to us the flame of fire of Jesus' baptism. We have all been baptized with water and with the Spirit. Our baptism into Jesus tells us we belong to Christ and we are members of His Church. Whether we were baptized as infants or as adults, it makes no difference. We are the Lord's. We want to be fired up for Jesus. We should not ashamed to be a Christian and to live for Christ. Everyone say, "I am hot for Jesus! I have the Holy Spirit, and the Spirit has me."

Lesson:
Jesus Is More Important Than Anyone   3 Advent (B)

Object: Shoe with a lace   **John 1:6-8, 19-28**

How many of you know how to tie a shoelace? Here is a shoe with the lace untied. Who would volunteer to tie the lace? Thank you. Well done! Once you know how, it is easy. I will tell you a secret. There is more than one way. I was once a paratrooper. They have a special way of tying the knot so it is not easily untied. When you are in a war, shoelaces are important.

Suppose I asked one of you to tie my shoelace? How would you feel about that? You might think it was sort of fun—especially if I showed you a super good way which made the laces stay tied. Then you could show the others how well you tie shoelaces. Tying laces might make you feel like a servant, too, as you have to kneel down before the person.

In the Gospel reading, we find a story of a great preacher named John the Baptizer. He was one of the most famous preachers of all time, but He said Jesus was much more important then he or anyone else. He said, "I am not worthy even to kneel down before Jesus and tie his shoelaces." That is how important he thought Jesus was. John was a fiery preacher. He even made some people afraid and some people were angry with him. But John was a humble man. He lived simply.

The Bible states that his clothes were very simple and plain, nothing fancy. His food was homegrown and tasty, he especially liked honey. Money was not his goal. He wanted to tell the whole world that a great leader was coming. That leader was Jesus. Jesus was so important and so great, John said, that to bow before Jesus or to help Jesus with His shoes was an honor. When you tie your shoes, remember that Jesus is your Lord and king.

Lesson:
Birth of Jesus Is Announced

4 Advent (B)

Object: Telegram or letter/of announcement of baby   Luke 1:26-38

Some mail is very special. It comes special delivery. For some letters, you must sign a card that says you have received it.

Years ago, important messages came by telegram. A messenger delivered it because the news was so important it could not wait. We live in a day when a telephone is usually available. I believe that one day soon, we will have phoni-vision. We will be able to see the person talking on a screen.

In our Gospel reading today, we have a story about the most important and exciting story in the history of the whole world. A young girl, not yet married, got a very surprising message. Who brought the message? A messenger! An angel named Gabriel.

He came saying, "Announcement, I have an announcement!" And what was it? That a very young woman named Mary was pregnant. Pregnant is a good word for you to know. It means that a woman is going to have a baby. This woman would have a baby boy. She knew it was a boy because the angel said so! The boy would be very special. He would be special because He was God's promised Son. Of course, every boy and girl is special to their mom and dad, but this baby was something else! A King!

The angel said, "He will be great and will be called the Son of the most High God, and the Lord will give Him a throne."

Mary even learned what the baby's name would be: Jesus.

"Don't be afraid," said the angel. "Jesus will be Lord and King." That was the message. When the angel spoke those words, you can be sure Mary wondered a lot. The Bible says, she "pondered" the words!—that is, she thought about them.

Lesson:
Jesus Was Born, the Word of God   Christmas (B)

Object: Blanket/soft, baby   John 1:1-14

Merry Christmas! What do I have to show you? Yes, a lovely baby blanket. What is a blanket like this used for? Of course, to keep a baby warm. I am sure Mary, the mother of baby Jesus, wished she had a nice, soft blanket for her newborn baby Jesus. Remember how the angel said to the shepherds, "Go to Bethlehem. You will find a baby wrapped in cloths and laying in a manger." Don't you think Mary and Joseph would have loved such a blanket.

The angel told the shepherds that Jesus was the Savior, sent as a baby by God himself. Some months later, the wise men came. They said Jesus was the King of the Jews, and would rule the whole world. Many years later, a man who followed Jesus as a disciple said Jesus was the Word of God. That's difficult to understand.

Here is a big question with no easy answer. "How does God come to us?" People have been asking this important question for a long time. Think about the answer. The blanket reminds us that God came in the form of Jesus, the babe of Bethlehem. John said, "God comes to us through the Word of God," meaning Jesus came as God in human form or God in the flesh, as a human being.

Jesus came to be present with us. That is the whole idea in this lesson. In some way, we have to know that God is present with us. Can we let this soft blanket remind us that Jesus is with us?

The Bible in the Gospel today has the words "dwelt among us." Maybe a better word is "lived among us." It means that God came to be present with us through Jesus in the power of the Holy Spirit. It is Christmas! Say this with me: "Jesus is the Word of God!"

Lesson:
Jesus Grew Up Like Us   1 Christmas (B)

Object: Scale/bathroom   **Luke 2:25-40**

The Gospel for this Sunday ends with this little paragraph: "When Joseph and Mary had finished doing all that was required, they returned to their hometown of Nazareth in Galilee. The child Jesus grew and became strong. He was full of wisdom and God's blessings were upon Him." Interesting! Revealing!

Jesus was born as a little baby, just like everybody else. We are all born as little babies. The Bible says Jesus was brought to the temple for dedication and blessing on the eighth day. A very old man who was there in the church to help with the ceremony had great words to say about the child Jesus. An old woman, too, spoke wonderful words about Him. I am sure Jesus' mother and father really wondered about these people who said such nice words about their baby.

Jesus had a family like us. There were his parents—Joseph and Mary, and later on there were more children in the family. As the years went by Jesus grew big and strong. Just like us! He put on pounds of weight.

While Jesus was growing up, He became strong and was full of wisdom. God's blessings were upon him. He went to school. I suppose there were times He didn't want to go to school, but He went anyway. Maybe there were some times, He didn't want to go to church, but He went anyway. Maybe there were times He didn't want to help around the house, but He did anyway, just like any one of us.

I wonder how people got weighed in Bible days? Scales had not yet been invented. Scales are rather new to our day. Bathroom scales are good to measure growth and weight. We don't know how Jesus got weighed, but we know He grew up, and He did what His Father wanted Him to do.

Lesson:
Meaning of Baptism

1 Epiphany (B)

Object: Shell or symbol of baptism

Mark 1:4-11

Today is a very special day in the life of our Lord. The symbol I have to show you is a shell (or a picture of a shell). The shell is an old symbol of baptism. Let us look at it carefully to get the meaning of what the shell wants to tell us about baptism.

What is the color? Blue. What does blue suggest to you? It is the usual color of water, and often helps us think of hope. Blue is a good color for baptism.

What is the color of the shield (the background)? Gold. Gold is a good color for beauty and richness, a precious color. It is a color that people have loved. Baptism is God's idea and precious, so gold is a good color to describe it.

How many drops of water are there on this shell (or in this picture)? Three. Why three? We are baptized in the name of God the Father, Son and Holy Spirit. How many of you have been baptized? If you were, you were baptized with water and the word of God. The word of the Lord is the promise that God will come to us and adopt us as His children. Your baptism is very precious. Baptism is God's work in us. God said to you and those who witnessed your baptism, "You are mine. You are my child. I put my claim on you. I want you to live your life for me."

Most people are baptized as babies. They don't even know it. They trust parents to take care of them, as we trust in God. Some children are baptized after they start school. Regardless of the age, baptism means that a person belongs to God. The Lord wants us to live in His grace. His grace comes through baptism.

Today, we celebrate Jesus' baptism by John the Baptizer in the Jordan River. God said to Jesus, "You are my beloved Son and I am very pleased with you." So, we have the promise of God just as Jesus had God's promise.

Lesson:
Watch for Surprises

2 Epiphany (B)

Object: Junk mail/advertisement

John 1:43-51

When you watch your mother and father open the mail, they throw some in the wastebasket. They might call it junk mail, like this one. Your parents may not even open it because they know it does not interest them. Or they do not want to know what it advertises. It is just a waste of time, so it is called junk mail.

What does this piece of junk mail have in it? This is telling about a sweepstakes. Do you think you could win a lot of money with it? Most people don't. They just throw it away. They think the time and effort to read it is a waste. To figure out the puzzles and the scratch offs are just too much. If you send it in, you have to pay the postage, too.

In the Gospel reading is a story something like all this junk mail. A man named Philip got excited about Jesus. Philip told his neighbor and friend Nathaniel about his excitement for Jesus.

Nathaniel blinked his eyes and shook his head. "Did you say he was from Nazareth? Why Philip, my friend, that is like getting junk mail. It is no good, my friend." Nathaniel was thinking to himself, no one keeps this stuff. It is like Nazareth, don't even give it a second thought. People were saying, "Can anything good come out of this little unknown town?"

Nazareth was a sleepy little place, not worth much. What would you compare it to? An old coal mining town? No one important comes from there. That is what Nathaniel might have said to his friend Philip. Well, he was wrong. What important person came from Nazareth? Jesus did! Sometimes that junk mail does mean something. Nathaniel was surprised. Always be ready for a surprise when Jesus is around!

Lesson:
Jesus Calls Us   3 Epiphany (B)

Object: Picture of five men   **Mark 1:14-20**

I have a picture of five men I want to show to you. I am wondering if we can decide who might be in this picture. Which one would be Jesus? The middle one? How would we know that? Because He looks like He is kind. That's a good answer. Sure, He looks good, and kind and gentle, as if He has authority, too. Who might these other four fellows be? Right. They are James and John and Peter and Andrew. These four boys are two sets of brothers. Simon Peter and his brother Andrew, and James and John, the sons of Zebedee, called the "sons of thunder."

Jesus had said, "I'm going to call them to be disciples." He would make them to be fishers of men. What does that mean? To be fishers of men? It means Jesus was going to teach them to use new ways to receive the Lord's blessing. They would fish for men, women and children. How could that be? It means that He was going to turn those nets into something like nets of love. He would use those men to bring other people to know that He was the Lord and the Savior. That's the Good News. That is what Jesus really does, even for us. He teaches us how to fish. That is how we use our love to bring others so that they come to know Jesus also as their Lord and Savior. He blesses them and multiplies their fish. He gives them lots of good things in life.

Look how fortunate we are. Do you see something really special about these four men? Do they look happy? Do you think they are proud to be with Jesus? We see them smiling and laughing and having a good time. They were very happy to be with Jesus, and we should be, too. We are proud to be able to fish with Jesus!

48

Lesson:
Jesus Wants Us Well   4 Epiphany (B)

Object: Thermometer   Mark 1:21-28

I am wondering how many of you have ever been sick. If you have been sick, raise your hand. Most of you have been sick. How do you know when you are sick? You have a stopped-up nose. You need rest. When you are really sick, when it hurts everywhere, you really know you are sick. Then you need one of these. A thermometer. What does it do? A thermometer is important because it tells us how sick we are. It tells us how much fever we have. We put it under our tongue for a few minutes.

But guess what? Thermometers also tell us when the fever is going away or gone. When fevers are gone, our body temperature is right, then we are ready for work and ready to play again.

Do you know that Jesus never had one of these to help heal people? Never! This is a new thing in the last century. Jesus' mother didn't have one of these either, did she? No! We do not know if Jesus ever got sick or not. My guess is that He did. He probably got sick just like we do.

Sickness is not God's idea. Not at all! God wants us to be happy and to be well, to have good health. That is His will for us. So He gives us doctors and nurses and hospitals and good medicine so we can be well. He wants us to be healed and to have good bodies that are not sick.

In the Gospel reading there is a lot about illness. The Gospel was about a man who had an evil spirit and got healed. That's another kind of illness. There are many different kinds of sicknesses. But we know from the Gospel that Jesus wants us well! Remember, Jesus is our healer. He brings us comfort.

Our Lives Can Be Healed 5 Epiphany (B)

Object: Cup/broken and reglued Mark 1:29-39

There are two things I want to show to you. This is glue. This very interesting cup is called a demitasse cup. It's a small after-dinner coffee cup.

This cup was accidentally dropped onto the floor and broke into pieces. You can see how it's been broken? We glued it together again. It looks good.

But look what happened on the inside. You can see all the cracks and lines where it has been broken. You can't drink out of this cup any more. It is together, but only for appearances. It is not like its new condition. When something breaks, it does not come together quite as nice as it was before.

The same is true with our lives. Our lives are something like the reglued cup. When our bodies and hearts get broken they can be healed, but they are not quite the same. Now, it's the Lord's will that all of our lives be healed because we have all been broken in some way or another. That is what sin does to us. But the Lord has provided a remedy. He put together the glue so that our lives could come together and be healed. Healing is God's work. Healing come through His love.

Today in our Gospel reading, we hear about Jesus' healing in the life of His disciple, Simon Peter and his wife who was sick with a fever. Sometimes, we have fevers and are sick. We need Jesus to heal us in our lives.

Today is the fifth Sunday of the Season of Epiphany. The Lord has revealed Himself to everyone, so that anyone who believes can be healed. Like this cup, the Lord can put us back together again. That is the meaning of Christmas, and the meaning of the cross, which comes to us as we begin to think about Lent. Forgiveness, love and healing come in the name of Jesus.

Lesson:
Jesus Makes Us New   6 Epiphany (B)

Object: Cloth/long strips, like gauze   Mark 1:40-45

I have these long pieces of white cloth. With them we will hear a
wonderful story of Jesus helping a very sick man. This man had
a disease called leprosy. It was a blood disease, which caused blood
circulation problems. Fingers would get blue, and the toes, too. It
was a bad disease, even the ears and nose were affected.

Because the disease was very contagious, anyone who had leprosy
had to stay away from others. Actually, they were supposed to notify
anyone close that a person with leprosy was nearby. The lepers made
a noise, or called out "leprosy," so that other people would stay away
and not get the disease.

Who would like to have these bandages on their arms and legs?
Who will volunteer? Good. Wrap your arms, your legs, some around
your neck and body. Oh, you look sick. Do you feel sick already? You
are sick!

A sick man got close to Jesus. He said, "You can make me clean."
Jesus touched him. Think about that! Here was this contagious disease which they believed could be passed on just by touching a person who had it. Yet, Jesus touched him. Jesus did a lot of touching.
He touched people in many ways. Jesus touched him, and that man
was made well. His skin was healed. Jesus wanted him to keep the
miracle a secret. But the man was so happy and excited, there was no
way for him to keep it a secret. He wanted other people to see and
know, too.

When Jesus makes you new, you get excited. When Jesus gives
you a new chance, you get real happy. Well, let's remove this cloth.
Don't you feel new and good and free from your disease? Everybody
say, "Yeah!"

Believe in the Lord

Object: mat/one used for sleeping   Mark 2:1-12

Years ago, a mat like this was used for sleeping. Even now in some places in the world, people use a mat like this as their bed. It is a mattress that you can carry. In the olden days it was called a pallet.

This Gospel reading is a favorite story of many. Jesus had been away and came home. Lots of people came to hear Him teach and preach. People were everywhere around Him, crowding into the front door of the house where He was staying. They wanted to see Jesus and hear Him teach and preach and heal.

One man could not walk. He laid on a mat like this. Others carried him where he wanted to go. It would be somewhat like people today who are pushed in wheelchairs or who lie on a moveable bed.

This paralyzed man wanted to see Jesus. His friends wanted to help him, but there was no way they could get in through the front door. Instead, they came through a window or opening in the roof. When Jesus saw their effort and faith, He said to the man, "Your sins are forgiven." The man was healed and began to walk.

Some people were really upset about Jesus' words. They thought sickness was the result of sin! Sometimes that is true. Sinful behavior can lead to an incurable illness, even paralysis as this man had. The bigger question was: Who gave Jesus the power and authority to forgive sins and heal diseases? Jesus had an answer for them. "What's the difference, to say 'Your sins are forgiven or to say, take your mat and walk'?" He asked.

The man who was paralyzed believed. He took his mat and walked. That's believing isn't it?! The idea is to believe in the Lord, to claim the Lord's promise, and do what the Lord commands!

Lesson:

Focus on Jesus   8 Epiphany (B)

Object: Cake/piece like wedding cake/cookie   Mark 2:18-22

---

*M*ost people believe in Jesus, but there are some who do not. They argue. They debate. They make excuses. We believe, so we come to church to sing and pray. We trust and obey and honor Jesus.

Some people seem to have a hard time believing that Jesus is Lord and Master. They want to be lord themselves and their own masters. They want to make their own rules. They are full of pride and selfishness.

One time, Jesus was with a group of people who argued. They accused Jesus' followers of breaking the law on the day of worship. Jesus thought their arguing and fighting was foolish. He gave them an example.

He said, "You don't mix new clothes and old coat. It would look funny. It would be out of place. Who would put on a new suit and a pair of shoes from the barn?" Then Jesus gave another example. "You don't put a new wine in an old container. It will burst." Would anyone put new milk in an old sour milk jar? No!

If you got a Cracker Jack box and it was empty, you would wonder. If you want a Hershey bar, and instead you got an old Baby Ruth, you would know it was wrong.

Jesus had said believing is like a wedding. The purpose is not to eat cake and drink coffee. Don't be foolish. Weddings are held for a man and woman to get married. The cake is extra. When you go to a wedding, there is food, like this cake (cookie). Do you expect the guests to go without food? Of course not!. They want to eat and have fun. So you provide the food and the fun. But the celebration is for the couple getting married, not the food. When we are with the Lord, we set our eyes on Him.

Lesson:
A Glimpse of God Transfiguration (B)

Object: Handkerchief/white, statue or picture of Jesus Mark 9:2-9

Transfiguration is a very important event in the life of our Lord. A great experience happened to Jesus and three of His disciples—Peter and the two brothers, James and John, on a high mountain. An experience which they never forgot. We call this happening the Transfiguration.

We don't know for sure what happened that day. One thing for certain, Jesus as a man had very close ties with God the Father in heaven. We get just a flashing look at what all of them saw and heard. Maybe it was something like this (white unfolded handkerchief placed over a little white statue of Jesus).

Jesus was there and a cloud came over and covered Him and the disciples. It was as if Jesus, really, turned back to His origins. He got a glimpse of God the Father from whom He had come. His face was bright, shining like the sun, and His clothes were dazzling white. He was talking with two of the great prophets, Moses and Elijah. Moses had led the people out of slavery from Egypt into the promised land. Elijah was the great prophet who had reminded the people they were a covenant people.

Maybe the scene looked something like this (remove the handkerchief). Jesus was dazzling white, beautiful and bright. The cloud came, covered them and was gone again. A beautiful experience for them!

Peter never forgot that he had been with Jesus on the mountain. He had seen Jesus transfigured. That's a strange, hard word. But it is the best word for this happening. Say it with me: Transfiguration!

Lesson:
Lent Is a Time for Prayer   1 Lent (B)

Object: Symbol of Lent   Mark 1:12-15

ent is a Latin word for spring, so Lent is always during spring-time. The forty days before Easter are called Lent. In Lent we thank the Lord for the joy that is ours because our sins are forgiven.

This symbol for Lent has the cup of the communion. The cup reminds us of the suffering of Jesus on the cross. The red lines are like His blood. The blue round symbol is like the world. Jesus came as a baby and died as a man for the sins of the whole world. Forgiveness comes to all who want to receive His love.

In the Gospel story, we understand that Lent begins with Jesus' temptation. Jesus was tempted by the devil to disobey God. Satan wanted Jesus to forget why He came into this world.

Purple is the color for Lent. During Lent, we set our minds on Jesus as our Lord. We lift up the cross. We focus on the cross and Jesus. We want to renew our faith. Faith is trust. Trust is a quality, which we build and grow.

Faith is also knowledge. We learn more about Jesus in Lent.

Another part of Lent centers on us. Jesus wants all people to be renewed in Lent, and to become an Alleluia people who praise the Lord. The symbol wants to say Alleluia! We let God see into our hearts. We want to be clean and pure before God. We confess our sins. We tell about our wrongs.

We are tempted, too. We usually know when we are tempted to sin. The devil is tricky. We want to pray and be smart and avoid his temptations. We want to pray and give thanks that the Lord keeps us strong. Prayer is a good way to do things for God in Lent. So let us pray:

"Lord Jesus, we pray, keep us from sin if possible. But when we do sin, we ask for Your forgiveness and the desire to do what is right. Amen."

Lesson:

Do Something Special in Lent for Jesus   2 Lent (B)

Object: Crucifix   **Mark 8:31-38**

In Lent, we do things for the Lord and for ourselves and for others, which are not usual. As an example, a man gave me this cross made out of old horseshoe nails and turquoise stones. I have chosen to wear it for Lent as a witness and reminder to me. It is called a crucifix. It has the body of Jesus on it.

When temptation comes, we look to the power of Jesus through the cross. We read and pray. Jesus gives us the power to resist every test and trial that the devil sends out way. Have all of you been tempted? Sure! And sometimes we give into temptation. That's when we need forgiveness, and the power to resist what we know is wrong. We want to be on the side of the Lord.

In our Bible story reading, Jesus asked us to "take up the cross and follow Him." The cross is not a magic wand. It is not a charm, which would keep hurt or evil away. For that reason, some people don't want to wear a cross at all. Other people wear a cross for fun, like it is a piece of jewelry. They wear the cross and yet they also sin. Some people carry a cross and steal. That is a sin. The fact is, everyone sins. The cross reminds us that there is sin and forgiveness.

My cross says I love Jesus, and I know He died for me and for my sin. We are to do something special for Lent. Some people give up some things for Lent. Instead, I have chosen to wear my cross and to pray in a special way for many people and for myself. I think on Jesus and remember that He did for me what I couldn't do for myself—save me and bring me the Lord's blessing. The Lord wants to give us all of the best that He has promised.

In Lent, we claim God's blessing by saying "yes" to Jesus. Remember this Bible story in which Jesus asks us to take up the cross. Lent is to think on Jesus!

Lesson:

Reverence for Worship   3 Lent (B)

Object: Hymn book/bulletin & envelope   John 2:13-22

I want to tell you a story about what happened one time when Jesus went into the temple. There were a lot of people there. Jesus got very upset with what He heard and saw happening in the temple. I want to tell you what that means for us and the lesson we can learn from this story.

You all know what a hymnbook is, don't you? It has all of our songs and the prayers. This is the bulletin for the order of service. This is an envelope to put your offering money in. What would you think if you came into church for worship, and somebody met you and your parents at the door and said, "You have to rent this hymn book. It's not free." Then they said, "You can't get a free bulletin from the ushers. You have to buy them." And when you brought your offering, they said, "Well, the kind of money you have won't work in this church. You have to have special money. We will exchange it for you. When we do, you have to pay extra." That's what was happening when Jesus came to the temple.

Jesus got very upset about the men's demand to pay extra money. The managers of the temple were overcharging and cheating right in God's house. Jesus was angry. He made a scene and got everybody's attention. He had a harsh word for them. He said, "You are making my Father's house into a marketplace. This is to be a place where we can come to worship and to praise God and to glorify Him. It is not a place for that kind of business."

It is like that for us, too. When we come to church, we want to be very reverent. We want to honor the Lord with quietness and respect. We want to know that this is the temple of the Lord, the place where we worship.

Lesson:
Lift High the Cross

4 Lent (B)

Object: Cross/processional (or make a 6"x1" cross)   John 3:14-21

We are in the middle of the time of Lent, the time to remember that Jesus suffered and died for us. Why was it necessary for Jesus to do that? The problem was with us. God came to our rescue. The devil had tricked human beings into sin at the beginning. Since then, everyone has had a problem with sin and the devil. God decided He would provide the remedy. The answer was Jesus on the cross. Lift high the cross.

The Bible reading tells us that God let Jesus be put on the cross so that He would be lifted up where people could see Him. That would tell how much God really loved us.

One night, Jesus was talking with a very smart man. In their conversation, Jesus told him a strange story from the Old Testament Numbers 21:9. Back then, the people of God forgot how much He cared about them, so He directed one of the leaders to put a metal carving of a snake on a pole and hold it high so everyone could see it. When the people looked at the carving, they were to remember that God was stronger than any snake who had bitten them. God promised that everyone who looked would be healed and saved. They were to be sorry for sinning against God. "They did look and believe," said Jesus. And they were healed and saved, and received a new promise.

When Jesus died on the cross, it was something like that. We look at the cross and remember Jesus. We remember that God so loved the world that He gave His Son Jesus. But some people today refuse to look on the cross. They are in big trouble, but they don't know it. Lift high the cross—and remember His love and care for us.

Lesson:
Die to Live   5 Lent (B)

Object: Stalk of wheat   John 12:20-33

W hat do I have here? A stalk of wheat. (Take out one grain of wheat) What is this? One little grain out of this head of wheat. See how small it is? Each head of wheat had many grains or kernels.

Jesus said in our Gospel story that if we take a grain of wheat and put it into the ground it begins to start a new plant. As that plant comes up, it forms a stalk of grain like this.

Once, farmers have seeded their grain, they watch their fields. One seed of wheat in good warm soil will sprout, and then spread out, forming two or three more stalks. Just think what will happen! How many grains there will be from one little grain. There are probably fifty to a hundred little grains in that one head of wheat. Think of the ratio, and how it multiplies. That is at least fifty to one.

Jesus said that His life, and our lives, are something like this little grain. It is good. It is strong. We are not just grain. We are special grain. We are clean grain. But how shall we understand this story as told by Jesus, because we are not grain? We are people.

How shall we understand that we are in some way like grain? I suggest this answer. We must risk loving somebody and showing kindness and tenderness. He wants our lives to be like this grain. It is good!

I believe Jesus knew He would die for us. He knew His life was like a grain of wheat. He knew that millions of people follow Him, like grains of wheat. That's the lesson to us. So then, let us multiply our love and kindness to other people so that wherever we are, we will live as unselfish people, just as Jesus gave His life unselfishly for us.

Lesson:
We Begin Holy Week   Palm Sunday (B)

Object: Branches, palm and garment   Mark 11:1-11

This last Sunday of Lent has two names. It is called both Passion Sunday and Palm Sunday. Palm Sunday is the day Jesus made His triumphal entry into Jerusalem. The people thought He was coming into the city to be the new king, the great messiah, coming to set Israel free from what they thought was slavery.

Can anyone tell me what I have here? Palm branches! Why do I have palm branches today? Yes! Because it is Palm Sunday.

God's chosen people had been in slavery and tyranny from the Roman Empire for many years. The people were not free. Taxes were heavy.

On Palm Sunday, Jesus rode into Jerusalem on a donkey. The people laid their coats and cloaks on the road. Others had palm branches that perhaps looked something like this. The reason they spread their clothing and branches was because they wanted to pro-claim that Jesus was the king who would free them. He was the messiah they had been awaiting for hundred of years.

This day is also known as the Sunday of the Passion. What does passion mean? It means suffering, and having lots of emotion. It has to do with Holy Week. People could not worship the way they wanted to worship. Worship is important. Is worship important for you and me? Surely! We prepare for worship carefully. We get up early. We dress up nice. We sing songs and read the Scriptures that have to do with Jesus' suffering on the cross. Today is a special day of preparation for Easter. The Sunday before Easter Sunday is always Palm Sunday and Sunday of the Passion.

Lesson:
New Life

Object: Lily/Easter

Mark 16:1-8

Several women went to the tomb very early to see where Jesus was buried. They were met by a young man dressed in white, like an angel. When they saw him, they realized Jesus was risen from death.

The white Easter lily tells us a story about resurrection. Notice the beautiful green color of the plant. Green is the color we usually connect with growth. We think of green leaves and flowers and the green grass. We know that means growth. So, the green of this plant tells us something about new life, doesn't it? And today we're talking about Jesus, who has risen from death into new life.

Easter is exciting because new life and hope comes through resurrection. Easter Sunday is very special for all of God's people. We are all dressed in our very nicest. We have come to a service of worship on Easter Sunday because Christ has risen. I want you all to say that with me. "Christ has risen." Once more. "Christ has risen."

That's what these flowers are saying as these white horns point in different directions. They are proclaiming to everybody that Christ has risen. The beautiful white color signified purity. They announce there is beauty, and that Christ has risen, indeed, from death. We praise the Lord for the power of the resurrection.

Lilies are placed in churches to make the inside look very pretty and give the whole room a lovely fragrance. When we smell the aroma and see the beauty of this flower, we want to get the deeper meaning, which is hope and love and forgiveness and new life.

Lesson:
Jesus Died/Rose/Celebrate

2 Easter (B)

Object: Candle/Paschal

John 20:19-31

One man came into a church and asked a question. He said, "Why is that red candle burning on the altar?" What would you say if someone asked you that?

"You know," I said, "when you have company for dinner in your home, you probably light candles. It is a kind of festive, special time. It's like that in the church, because Jesus is present with us.

In the Gospel reading, we have the story of Jesus being present with the disciples after resurrection. The doors were locked because the followers of Jesus were afraid. But Jesus came through the locked doors. He said, "Peace to you." Jesus showed them the wounds and hurts he had suffered on the cross.

This candle is called a "paschal" candle—a candle of suffering—to remind us of Jesus' death.

Jesus said again, "Peace to you." It's a special time, when we come together to worship, so we light this candle to celebrate Resurrection. But there is something else about all the candles. Candles remind us of light. If this room was dark and we lit one candle, you could probably see enough to find your way around. If you put your hand near one of those candles, you would feel its warmth.

We're talking about love, and love is like light and warmth. Love helps us see things we didn't see before and to believe things we didn't believe before. Love is warm. It makes us feel warm and good when we receive love and get love. Listen very carefully to the Journey of Love as Jesus' resurrection continues to be celebrated.

Lesson:
Jesus Is with Us   3 Easter (B)

Object: Picture/Jesus with children   Luke 24:36-49

Pretend that we can ask Jesus what happened to His hands and that He will tell us. He has a big scar in His hands. How did those sores get there?

"It looks like somebody tried to hurt you," a girl is saying to Jesus. "Were you climbing in the tree? Did you jump off the swing and land on the ground and get hurt?"

Jesus said to her, "Some men hurt Me. See the holes in My hands? They drove nails through them when I was crucified. See My feet? They put nails there, too."

Jesus came to His followers after His resurrection. He wanted them to know that He could now be present with everyone—anytime, anyplace. Jesus said to them, "Why do questions arise in your minds? Do you have anything here to eat?" The followers were totally confused.

Jesus knew what He was doing. He wanted them to know God was near them, and that Jesus would be in every believer in the power of the Holy Spirit. Instead of being with just a handful of people, He would now be with all the people who believed in Him, who received Him as the resurrected Lord.

Jesus is very real in our lives. This is a very beautiful picture of Jesus, and the resurrection, and gathering the children around Him. He also wants us to gather around Him. He wants us to know that He is the real Lord, Jesus Christ.

In the Gospel reading, Jesus opened His disciples' minds to understand the Scripture and the power of His name. He wanted them to understand that He lives again and can be with them all. Say with me, "Jesus lives." Once more: "Jesus lives!"

Lesson:
Be a Good Shepherd

Object: Staff/Shepherd's

In the Gospel reading, we have a story of Jesus as the good shepherd. He said, "I am the good shepherd." A shepherd is a person who takes care of sheep when the flock is out in the pasture. The shepherd herds the sheep. The word shepherd comes from sheepherder.

It is very important that the shepherd be careful with every sheep. None are to be lost. They must be counted every day. If one is gone, it must be found before the day is over. The shepherd will even leave the flock to find a lost sheep who has strayed away from the others.

One time, Jesus told a story about a lost sheep. There were one hundred sheep. The shepherd counted ten on his fingers, ten times. One sheep was missing. Ninety-nine were in the flock. He looked until he found the one who strayed away to have fun. When the shepherd found the lost sheep, Jesus said everyone rejoiced and laughed. A good shepherd was responsible and careful. He had a job to do and he did it well. The good shepherd would be willing to die for the sheep. That is exactly what Jesus did for us on Good Friday.

Every shepherd has a staff like this one. With a staff, the shepherd could guide the flock. He could rescue a lamb. He could drive away a wolf. He could help the sheep grow and be strong and safe.

Sometimes we are like sheep and sometimes we are like the shepherd. We need help and we give help. Jesus is our helper who takes care of us and watches over us. We must want to be in His flock. When we see other people hurting, we can be a shepherd to them. We can comfort them when they cry. We must be good sheep and obey, and also be a good shepherd and help!

Lesson:
Live and Bear Fruit

5 Easter (B)

Object: Branch/grape vine/one fresh, one dried up

John 15:1-8

The Gospel reading says that if a vine is cut off from the branch, it will soon dry up. It gets ugly and withered, and pretty soon we can just throw it away. That's the end of it. It is good for nothing! Here is a sample. This branch was nice and green this morning, but I cut it off the vine, and now it is dried up and dead. Worthless. This vine is so useless that it is not even any good for firewood. It just goes poof!

The point here is that a branch has to remain on the vine to be green and beautiful. Then it will be nice and green and beautiful, and eventually in the late summer or early fall, there will be nice grapes on it. The grapes will be sweet and lovely, and we enjoy them very much.

What does this mean for us? We are like the branches on the vine! We live in Christ. He is the vine. If we stay on the vine we will bear fruit. The fruit is that we are full of joy in our own lives, and we help others to be joyful people. People are happy and living in the Lord because they know God's Word and share together in prayer. We want to share our love and our joy with as many people as we can. That's what it means to abide in Christ and His Church.

If we do not stick with the Lord and His Church, we look like this cut-off vine. We are not useable. We will produce nothing. God wants more than green leaves and lots of vines. What does God want? He wants grapes. Of course! What are grapes for? Eating. For grape juice. For grape jelly. For the good things in life.

Jesus wants your life to bear fruit. That means your life has a purpose and a meaning. Let your life be like a strong branch of the vine, a good green grape-producing vine.

Joy Comes from Love

Object: Sign/Joy

*J*esus said that if we remain in Him, like grapes cling to the vine, we can ask for favors from the Lord. In our Gospel story for today, Jesus goes further with this promise. He taught the disciples that just as grapes and vines hang together, so does love and joy. Love is a wonderful gift to give to each other, and to receive. One of the things that comes out of love is joy. Joy is a wonderful feeling. It is like pleasure. It is like a truckload of happiness.

I have a sign (acrostic) that has the letters J O Y. We know it is a word which means happiness and fun and gladness. Joy goes along with love. Love and joy are buddies.

Jesus said that good friends will share their love and joy with each other. Let us look at joy and see what good words we can fill in with each letter of the word. Each of you look at my sign. Think about love. Think about Jesus. Think about others. Remember that one of Jesus' great teachings was to love others before ourselves.

So, what shall we put for "J"? Whose name are we talking about that would best go with "J"? Of course, J for Jesus. We want to put Jesus first in our lives. We know that love and happiness come from Him.

What about the letter "O"? After Jesus, who comes next? How about "others"? We are to love and serve others.

So, who would be the "Y"? Well, why not us (you and me) for the "Y"? Surely. You are important. The order of priority is correct. Jesus, others, and you. That's the secret of joy. Now all of you know the way to have joy. Joy comes through love.

Lesson:

We Are Not Forgotten

Object: Photo/two small children

John 17:11-19

Have you ever been lost? Anyone who has been lost, even for a few minutes, knows how anxious you can feel. Even when you are with your parents and you go exploring in a store, you can get that lost feeling. Your parents can be close at hand but maybe you can't see them because someone gets in the way. That's when you can get scared. Parents are very important when it comes to fear. The world is big. When we are small, everything seems very big.

Here is a picture of two children. Do you see a mother and a dad in the picture? No, only the children. However, you imagine with me that the parents are behind the children. The parents are there but we can't see them. Are the children lost? No, because they look happy. Are they afraid? Not yet!

Jesus prayed in our Gospel reading that we would all be safe. His prayer was that we be safe from the evil one. We know that the devil is out to get us. We are not spared. We are not vaccinated against the devil, but we do have power over the devil in the name of Jesus. When you are being tested with anything bad, think about Jesus. He will provide you with good thinking and strength. It is like your mother and dad are present in the picture, but you cannot see them. However, you know they are present. So also is Jesus!

"We are in the world," Jesus said. And we must stay in the world because that is where God wants us to be. We are in the world so we can share love with the world. But we are not to be of the world (I John 2:15-17). The children are enjoying the world and Jesus has prayed that we be kept safe from the evil one. That means the devil. Jesus is like our parents. When we are near Jesus, we are safe and we feel secure. We can be strong in our faith and able to resist evil.

Lesson:
We Are the Church
Pentecost (B)

Object: Letters/C H U R C H
John 7:37-39

Red is the color for Pentecost Sunday. Pentecost is a strange word. But that's what it is today—Pentecost Sunday. Today is the birthday of the Christian church, fifty days after Easter. Jesus promised in the Gospel that "those who believed in Him were to receive the Spirit."

On the day of Pentecost, the Holy Spirit was given to the church and to us. The Spirit fills us with grace and faith, making us into believers. As empowered believers, we show that we have the fruits of the Spirit by how we live, and we share the gifts He gives with everyone in the church.

We have four things! Pentecost, the Spirit, the Church, and its birthday. What is the church? Of course, the church is buildings, pastors, and worship.

However, the most important thing about the church is the people of God who are the church, and they receive the gifts promised by Jesus Himself.

Today we want to show one another what it means to be the church. Will you two girls stand up please and hold these two letters "CH" for me? We've got the beginnings of CHURCH. Now, will you two boys stand up please and take the other letters "CH"? Now we've got the letters CH and CH. What's missing? Two letters. You take this letter which is a "U", and you take this other letter which is an "R". Now let's add these two letters. What does it say? It says CHURCH. If we don't have those two letters in the word, what's missing? U R! So, if you don't come to church, U R missing! It's very important that U R here.

Pentecost tells us that the people of God come together in the power of the Holy Spirit to form the church, which is the body of Christ. Let us praise God because it is important that U R here for worship and praise.

Lesson:
Trinity/Three-in-One God   Trinity Sunday (B)

Object: Candles/three   **John 3:1-17**

Today is Holy Trinity Sunday. We are going to talk about God. There is one God. He is our Lord. The object for our lesson are the three candles lighted on the altar. What do they represent? Answer: Father, Son and Holy Spirit. One and one and one makes how many? Three!

In the church we say one and one and one is One. Isn't that something? Did you ever think about that? We have God the Father, God the Son and God the Holy Spirit. Yet, we say there is one God. That's a mystery! That's a mathematical mystery. Everybody has struggled and had lots of problems with the word Trinity. All through generations from the days of Jesus and even on until now, children and adults have had difficulty in understanding God. Three candles on the altar, but only one God. Remember the word mystery when you hear the word Trinity.

A man came to Jesus for information. He wanted to know God and the miracles which Jesus did. The man asked, "How could you do all these things? They are a mystery to me." Jesus said, "If you understand the meaning of the water and the Spirit, you will know the secret of the mystery." But do you know what? The man could not understand Jesus' teaching of being born again, any more than we understand Trinity.

Finally, Jesus said, "Remember that Old Testament story about the snakes that bit people? God healed them. That was a mystery, too." It is just like believing the symbol of the cross. Believing about Jesus on the cross is mystery. Believing in the name of God, the Father, Son and Holy Spirit takes faith. The secret of mystery is to believe. That's what Jesus told the man, and that's why we have three lighted candles. Believe, children, believe.

Lesson:
We Begin to Prepare for Jesus
1 Advent (C)

Object: Advent Wreath

Luke 21:25-36

You know something different is being celebrated because we have an Advent wreath. How many candles are on this wreath? Four. One for each of the four Sundays of Advent. There are three white ones. The fourth is often an old fashioned pink candle. This pink candle is called the Bethlehem candle, and it is to be lighted the third Sunday. If you have a modern-day wreath, you might have four blue candles. The color is blue for the four Sundays in Advent.

You can make a wreath like this at home. Maybe you can make a wreath with some greens in a small circle. Use four candle holders and four candles, and light one each Sunday. Because today is the first Sunday of Advent, you would light one today. Next Sunday, the second one, and so on, with the last one being lit on the fourth Sunday of Advent.

Then it's Christmas. As you light each one, sing a Christmas song like "Away in the Manger" or "Silent Night" or "Joy to the World." I suggest that you ask your mother and dad to tell you about Mary and Joseph, and ask about Elizabeth, too.

The Bible tells us about Mary and Joseph in the Gospel of Luke, chapters 1 and 2. We prepare for Jesus in Advent. It is the time we remember that Jesus is coming again. He came once, and He will come again. We are to be prepared and waiting for His return. He comes for us as persons, and He will come again for us as a Church and for all the people of God.

Watch and pray and rejoice! Advent is the time we prepare for the coming of the baby Jesus, who is born to be our Lord and Savior.

Lesson:

Be Ready for Jesus to Come

2 Advent (C)

Object: Sign/U turn permitted?

Luke 3:1-6

How many of you can read signs? We see a lot of signs. Crosswalk, Stop, Go, Listen or School Crossing. What is a U-turn sign? It means you can go back the same way you came. Change direction. Turn the car around. Return.

A sign that said "U-Turn Permitted" would be unusual. Why would anyone put up such a sign? Where? Maybe where a turnoff was easily missed, or where the road seemed to end.

In the Gospel story there is a strange man named John who said it is okay to make U-turns. John was trying to get people ready for Jesus to come. He knew that people were not ready so he said to them, "Make a U-turn and get ready. Go back." Of course, John was not talking about roads and cars. There were no cars in those days. People walked or rode on a donkey.

John was talking about people and their lives. People were sinning in many ways. They cheated on taxes. They drank too much wine. People got killed. Some were angry. Some people hated their neighbors.

John was saying, "Deal with sin. Ask the Lord to guide you. Get forgiveness. Be ready for Jesus."

We know that John was a strange man with weird ideas, as far as the people of that day knew. He just did not fit the pattern and life of those people. People would shake their heads, blink their eyes and look away in disgust. John even dressed crazy and ate unusual food.

Children! Christmas is almost here, so get ready for the coming of baby Jesus. Watch for the signs that show Jesus is soon to be born.

Lesson:
There Is a Clean and An Unclean Part of Us

3 Advent (C)

Object: Flour Sifter

Luke 3:7-18

I have a gadget from our kitchen to show you. What is this utensil called? A sifter! Correct. Cooks use it to sift flour. Sometimes flour has lumps in it. A drop of water can cause a lump to form, or rice could fall into the flour bin. No one wants to eat a kernel of rice or bite into a hard lump in bread, or cake or cookies. So, cooks sift the flour until it is pure and clean.

Sometimes our lives need to be sifted, too. We have a clean part of us. But we know there is also an unclean part inside of us. That unclean part we call sin. Sin comes into our minds and hearts. Sin is in everybody. No one escapes sin. It is something we are, and something we do. Both! We are sinful in some things we do and say.

When we hurt someone on purpose, it is a sin! When we say something nasty, it is sin. Sin is with and in all people all the time, and has been from the beginning of time.

In our Gospel story, John the Baptizer is telling the people about good and bad. John didn't have a flour sifter, but there was a device called a winnowing fork that was something like it. It sifted out good wheat seeds, and let the hulls blow away. John the Baptizer came preaching repentance. Repentance means a U-turn is permitted. But there is another side in all of this. God wants the very best for us. He wants to sift out the bad part so we can love and serve Him better and each other, too. The sifted flour is like our love. It is good for making bread or cookies. The lumps and hard pieces of flour are like the sinful things we do and say. God wants us to clean up our lives, so that we can get all the best He has for us.

Lesson:

Appreciate Mary

4 Advent (C)

Object: Picture/A beautiful woman, veiled if possible   Luke 1:39-55

I am sure you are excited. What event is coming in just a few days? The Gospel story tells us that Christmas is close at hand.

I have a picture to remind us of the coming birth of Jesus. Who can tell me who this woman might be? How many say it is Mary? Very good! It *is* Mary!

When you see a picture of Mary, how do you feel? Sweet. Good. Nice. Special. Surely, we all think Mary was special. Everybody loves Mary, God's special woman.

Before Mary knew that she would give birth to baby Jesus, she was just like any ordinary young girl. God can use anyone in a special way. God selected Mary for a special reason—to be the mother of Jesus.

Mary went to visit her cousin Elizabeth. She said to Mary, "You are blessed among women." That means, "Mary, you are really lucky that the Lord has picked you. You will be blessed and you will bless many people." Mary is a part of Christmas, because Mary was the mother of Jesus. Jesus was the Son of God.

We do not know why God chose Mary. There are many "whys" we can never answer. For example: why has God permitted you to be born? And, to live in America? And, to believe in Jesus as your Lord? Or, to live with a wonderful mother and father? You will never know why! It makes no difference. All we know is that God permitted Mary, a very young girl, to be the mother of the Lord Jesus. We want to appreciate her! She was singled out by God for a special task and for a special reason. Mary was obedient to the Lord!

Lesson:
Meaning of Christmas

Christmas Day (C)

Object: Crèche/Manger Scene

Luke 1:1-20

We are celebrating Christmas. Let us look at this crèche—a manger scene. Who are these people? The shepherds. They had been out in the fields watching the flocks. What else it there? Animals. There was no place in the inn, so Joseph and Mary went to the next best place for shelter, a place where animals were kept. There may have been birds and chickens and ducks, too.

Mary and Joseph had come to Bethlehem, which was their hometown, to be counted in the census. The king, called a Caesar, was not concerned about the number of people, but he did want to know who could pay taxes. Joseph had to report to be counted.

Baby Jesus was born, and an angel said to the shepherds that there was really good news in Bethlehem. They knew what to search for because the angel told them to look for a new baby lying in a manger. A manger is like a big feedbox with hay and straw that cattle eat from. There was baby Jesus, lying in that big feedbox.

Remember, it was the olden days. Not like our day. There were no hospitals in those days. Babies were born at home, or wherever they decided to come. What is your favorite Christmas song? One of mine is "Infant Holy, Infant Lowly," The words are "…for his bed a cattle stall. Christ the child is Lord of all." In the song "Silent Night," the words say, "Jesus, Lord, at Thy birth; Jesus, Lord, at Thy birth." That's the meaning of Christmas: Jesus has come to be the Lord!

Lesson:
Grow with the Lord

1 Christmas (C)

Object: Stick/Cubit

Luke 2:41-52

*I*n our Gospel story we read about Jesus as a young boy about age 12. His family had been in worship in Jerusalem. They were a long way from home. It would be like you went to Grandpa and Grandma's house many miles away for church. For Jesus' family, it would have been a four- to five-day walk.

The event was a very special day of the year for worship called the Passover. Passover was a really fun time, like the Fourth of July, Thanksgiving Day and a big birthday party all in one day or week. The people walked all the way to and back from their church which was called a temple.

When Passover was over, Jesus stayed behind. Mother thought Jesus was with His dad, and Joseph thought Jesus was with His mother. Actually, Jesus had stayed to discuss some things with the people in the temple. Finally, after a frantic search, His parents found Him and they went home.

The Bible says, "Jesus grew and became strong." Sometimes, we measure ourselves to see how much we are growing. I have here a measuring stick that was standard in Jesus' day. It is one cubit long, or 17 1/2 inches. Who is twelve years old? Let's measure you and see how tall you are. Would you stand, please? That's maybe how tall Jesus was when He got left behind in the temple.

To grow up is important. The Bible reading says, "Jesus grew in wisdom, gaining favor with God and man." We are to grow in God's favor, too. That means to be smart about God. Learn to pray, even out loud. Learn to sing nicely. Learn good manners. Keep the commandments. Manage your time and money. Grow wiser every day. In other words, grow up in the Lord.

Lesson:
Meaning of Baptism　　　　　Epiphany/Baptism (C)

Object: Baptismal Cloth　　　　　　　Luke 3:15-17, 21-22

Thank you for coming to children's time. I have this little piece of cloth. Who thinks they know what this cloth is? When would we use a beautiful cloth like this? Baptism. That is correct! When we have baptism, the water is placed on the head of a child, and we wipe the baby's head with this towel. On the bottom of the cloth is embroidered a little cross. The cross reminds us that the baptism is God's work. It's God's way of bringing us His grace.

Today in the church calendar year we celebrate a very special Sunday. It is called the Baptism of Jesus Sunday. Jesus came to be baptized in the Jordan River by a man named John. Jesus was baptized before He went out to teach the people about God. We know that Jesus did not have any sin, so really, He did not need to be baptized. So why do you think He came to be baptized by John? This is a very hard question. I will tell you why. He wanted the people of that day to know, and He wanted us to know, that something very special was to begin. He was beginning His ministry.

Because Jesus was baptized, He received a renewal promise from God. The words of the promise were "You are my beloved son, and I am delighted with you." Jesus knew He had God's favor. So also, we are made clean and assured of the promise that God is very pleased with us. We have His favor. To symbolize that washing, we have this white soft cotton baptismal cloth. It tells us that God has given the promise of His Word so that we know Christ's love, symbolized for us by this piece of cloth.

In the Gospel for today, this event is called the Baptism of Jesus. There are many things for you to learn about Jesus and His baptism. And there will be many things for you as you learn the meaning of baptism and Jesus' work for us.

Lesson:

Be Obedient

2 Epiphany (C)

Object: Wedding Invitation

John 2:1-11

I have a card. It's not a Christmas card. You can see that it's not a birthday card. What is it? This is a wedding invitation card.

This card happens to be one that was sent out by my wife's father. It says, "William Westman requests the honor of your presence at the marriage of their daughter, Bernell." Bernell is my wife.

Invitations are sent out for a wedding because weddings are a lot of fun. They're fun because we celebrate. But weddings are also serious because two people are saying to one another—they are going to live together for the rest of their lives, in unity and in thankfulness for each other. People spend much money to get married. They invite lots of people and have lots of food. They buy lovely clothes. How many of you girls want nice lacy, satin and silky white wedding dresses? Great!

Jesus was invited to a wedding. At this wedding they ran short of beverages, so Jesus took some water in the big drinking jars and turned the water into table wine. Everyone knew it was a miracle.

But Jesus could not do the miracle alone. Others worked with him. These servants helped Jesus so that He could perform the miracle. That meant they had to be obedient. Do what was asked, no questions! Obedience is very important. What does obedience mean? It means to obey. To do what you're told or asked to do.

What I want you to learn from this lesson is that it is good and right to be obedient. The Lord wants us to be obedient. Jesus is going to continue to work through us as His people, so we want to be obedient to Him.

We Are the Church

3 Epiphany (C)

Object: Word/Church/People/Synagogue

Luke 4:14-21

I want to show you a word? This word is CHURCH/PEOPLE. We know what church is, don't we? We go to church, meaning a place to worship. We have church, meaning singing and praying. I have a question: Do you think Jesus went to church? "Yes," says the Bible. It says, "…as it was usual for Him to do." That means, going to worship was customary and Jesus did it all the time.

But, in Jesus' day, people didn't call it church. They had a different word. The word is this big, long word. (flip side of word church/people) SYNAGOGUE. It's a place where they went to teach, like going to Sunday school class. They had a lot of singing and reading of the Scriptures from the Old Testament, and they had worship time.

We might say that the synagogue was a fun place. The children came, and played, and laughed together. When we can combine teaching and worship with fun and play, then we are spiritual beings made strong. Work with no play is no fun. People worship. Worship is for everyone.

Jesus was in his hometown church. He was asked to read the lessons from the Bible. He read from the prophet Isaiah and said, "This Scripture is come true today." Everybody was very surprised, wondering what it meant. It meant the good news was beginning to be spoken. It was the beginning of the church. Jesus wanted to teach us a lesson about church.

The church is not only a place, but it is people. It is you and me. We are the church. Will you repeat these words after me: "I am the church. You are the church. We are the church together." Now, everybody say it. "I am the church. You are the church. We are the church together." It is worship by God's people—US! You and me!

Lesson:
People Know Us By Our Behavior   4 Epiphany (C)

Object: Passport   Luke 4:21-32

*J*esus was in His home church, reading the Scriptures and teach-ing the people. Somehow, they knew who Jesus was. We know that Jesus grew up in Nazareth, His hometown. But as He got older, some wondered about Him. He has changed. He is different. He does not seem like the same little boy. Is He the same person? Can this be the boy we knew as a teenager? These words could be also true for us as we get older. Oh, how true!

I have a little book. Can anyone read what it says? Passport. If I were to go to another country, they wouldn't know who I am. They couldn't tell if I was a Christian, or not a Christian. But they would know my name because they would see my name and the picture. They would know that the person who had this book is me. It's my passport.

Jesus didn't have a passport. People knew who He was because of what He told them, and by how He lived. How we live and what we say become very important, because that is the way people know who we are, unless we carry a passport all the time. We can tell peo-ple our name. But when they see what we do and hear what we say, they know what kind of people we are. The song says, "They will know we are Christians by our love." It's true that I don't need this passbook if I'm going to go to New Mexico or New York or to Minnesota. I do not need this book because we have the freedom to travel. In many countries we don't have that freedom. People only know we are Christians by how we speak and by what we do. So it becomes very important that we live our lives for the Lord. I know you want to live for the Lord. It is not always easy, but it is great! When we live for the Lord, we are promised His blessing!

We Are to Tell the (Fish) Story

5 Epiphany (C)

Object: Symbol/fish and letters JESUS

Luke 5:1-11

I have a symbol I want to show you. Can you see the outline of this symbol? What does it look like? Yes, it is a fish. These letters J-E-S-U-S are shaped so they look like a fish.

The fish is one of the most ancient symbols in the Christian Church. From the very beginning, from Jesus' time, this was the symbol that stood for Jesus. The symbol of the fish also stood for people who followed Jesus.

In the olden days, before paper and pencils, before computers and graphics, people had other ways to make a sign or to tell someone what they believed. Long ago, to be a follow of Jesus was dangerous, and the people had some tricky ways of telling about their faith, so no one would know it.

Here is an example: They would take their finger or a toe and draw in the sand a picture of a fish. (Word JESUS in the shape of a fish.)

Jesus used the word "fish" to mean people as well as fish. So the symbol has a double meaning. It meant fish, but it also meant Jesus. Sometimes you will see this symbol on the back of a car or in a house. Any time you see it, you know it stands for Jesus.

When you hear the Gospel story, it will tell you about Jesus calling people to go and tell others the Good News. We are to tell the fish story! We are to talk with people and to touch them. That's what Jesus wants you to do.

This symbol wants to remind us that we are to be fishermen for Jesus. We do that by telling others about Jesus. We can take somebody by the hand and say, "Come with me to Sunday school or to my church." This symbol tells us who we are. We are Jesus' people.

Lesson:
Jesus Wants Us to Be Happy   6 Epiphany (C)

Object: Globe   Luke 6:17-26

A globe tells us that there are many lands and seas in the world. There are many kinds of people. They have different color skin and hair and eyes. However, there are some things that all people have in common. Think about the Chinese. Now Mexicans. Now Norwegians. Now Americans. What is the same for all of them? All people are born. And all people die. All have to eat, sleep and breathe air. And everybody likes to be loved!

Jesus has one great purpose. He wants all people everywhere to believe in Him. He wants people to know that sins can be forgiven, and that people can all be happy. Does it make any difference where they live? No! Not at all. Does skin color matter? No! Not at all.

Is everyone a good friend of everyone else in the world? No. It seems someone is always at war someplace. A friend is someone you like. A friend is someone you trust. There are people who don't trust—nor do they like—others. Sometimes these people take advantage of others. They cause war and have people killed. The reason is usually power and money. It was true in Jesus' day and it's true for us, too.

Jesus said in our Gospel reading that He wants us to be happy, or blessed. Those two words have nearly the same meaning. Can we be happy when things go wrong? It's not so easy, is it? When someone hurts you, it is not easy to be happy. When you are sad, you are not happy!

The world is like the globe. Jesus came into this whole world, because God had the idea that we should be happy. When we are saved, we are happy. When we love Jesus, we are blessed. We are commanded to take the Good News of Jesus and God's love to all people all over the world!

Lesson:
Jesus Gives Us Full Measure

Object: Apron with large front

Luke 6:27-38

This piece of cloth looks like what? A shirt. That's close. An apron. Good. What are aprons used for? To help a mother or dad keep their nice clothes cleaned in the kitchen. An apron is a garment for protection of spilled foods. In the olden days, the women wore aprons just like mothers and dads do today.

In this Lesson, Jesus is talking about love and our enemies, about people who might not like us very much. "Pray for your enemies," Jesus said. He said we should be careful about judging people.

He remembered how a woman could form a basket in her apron by folding up the corners. She could carry a whole apron full of things from the garden like peas, or grapes, or oranges.

Jesus said, "Instead of hating the people who don't like you, and putting them down, give and it will be given to you, full measure." That's like an apron full.

If you have candy, share it. Give some of it to someone you might not want to give to, and much will be given to you. Jesus gives full measure. It is like having an apron full of good things.

The Lord wants the best for each of us. You must be willing to share and help others. Do good to them. If someone gets the best of you, don't go for revenge. Maybe the person who gets candy from you is not your best friend, but he might be someday. If someone takes one of your suckers, you say to that person, "Here now, would you want this one, too?" If someone kicks you, don't kick back. If someone bites you on the hand, don't bite back. Instead say, "That biting hurts me! Jesus is not pleased that you hurt me."

Jesus said, "Give love and forgiveness and love will be given you."

Lesson:

Build a Strong Faith

8 Epiphany (C)

Object: Stone/several pieces of

Luke 6:39-49

*J*esus once said that anyone who listens to Him, and comes to Him, is like a very strong building. Buildings have to be strong in all kinds of weather—cold and snow, rain and hail, or terribly hot. One time Jesus said, "The rains came, and the wind blew and stormed. But the house stood firm." The bottom part of the house was made out of stone like this (a piece of stone).

Jesus said, "Everyone who comes to me is like a person who builds a strong house. Everyone who hears my word and does them is like a person who dug deep and laid a solid foundation for that building."

What does this mean for us? Build a strong faith for your life like a house. Your life needs a foundation that is like this stone. Jesus was talking about solid rock. What did He mean? What makes us strong? What are the good stones?

I think He meant love. Surely He meant to pray and sing. To forgive, that's a big stone. Sharing and caring for each other is another big stone. Worship, that's a really big stone. All of these are good.

When you are home, ask your mother and dad about good stones. Have your dad show you how well your house is built. Look at the cement and foundation. Look at the outside. See the garage and the attic.

Ask your mother how your faith is like some parts of the house. Can you make a cake without a pan and baking oven? What are the good stones in your kitchen? How are they like your life?

The Bible says Jesus is our precious stone. In another place, the Bible says that no other foundation can anyone lay than Jesus. Build a strong faith on a good foundation.

Lesson:
We Would See Jesus   Transfiguration (C)

Object: Popcorn/Box or basket or paper bag   Luke 9:28-36

In the Gospel story, James and John and Peter were with Jesus on a mountain. They were having fun together the way we might do when we are having popcorn with family and friends at a movie.

But they became fearful. Something happened which changed fun into fear. They saw Jesus talking with some men who had died a long time ago. Everything became mysterious and strange. Jesus seemed to be talking with God. The disciples were afraid. This was a wonderful, yet fearful place to be.

Peter said, "I'll build three tents, one for each of you—Moses, Elijah and You, Jesus, and we'll just stay here. We are not going to leave. We are just going to stay right here on the mountaintop, because it is so beautiful."

Just like they were having lots of popcorn and lots of fun, they didn't want to go home. They wanted to stay there as long as they could. Yet, they were so afraid they didn't even know what to say.

We don't know for sure what Peter's words meant. They might not have made a lot of sense because he didn't really know what to say.

Sometimes when we are having a lot of fun and there is excitement, we don't know what to say. It is like having a big bag of good popcorn. Maybe you think there really is not any popcorn in this box (a bag). There really is! Would you like to eat some?

This Gospel story talks about a mountaintop experience of change called Transfiguration. Something beautiful and wonderful happened to Jesus and the three disciples. Our lesson is difficult to understand, so you might have to ask your mom and dad to help you with the story when you have popcorn with them.

Lesson:
Cross Tells of God's Love

Object: Cross/Lent

Luke 4:1-13

Today is the first Sunday in Lent. Lent is a very special time of the year. In Lent we center our attention on the cross and on the work Jesus did for us at the cross. There are some things we want to do in Lent which we might not otherwise do. One of them is to think about Jesus and to remember the cross.

I have this very special cross I wear only for Lent. Can you see how it is different? The body of Jesus on the cross reminds us of Jesus' human sacrifice. This is called a crucifix. The cross is made from nails.

The crucifix is a constant reminder that Lent is the time you think about Jesus. When you have your evening prayer with your mother and dad, or you have bedtime prayers, think on Jesus and remember the cross. We set our minds on Jesus, we rest in Jesus, and we relax in Jesus for our sleep.

In our Gospel reading, we have the story that Jesus was tempted by the devil, but He resisted. Jesus did not let the devil fool Him with any distraction. The devil showed Jesus some very nice things that could have made Jesus feel good, but Jesus knew the devil was tricky, so He kept His mind on God. The devil has many ways to tempt us. Most of the time he uses things that are very common. Example: There may be money on a dresser in a bedroom and you are tempted to snitch some of it. Resist! Or you may be shopping and the temptation is to put some gum or candy in your pocket. Big temptation. Resist! Instead, think of Jesus and remember the cross.

When temptation comes to us, whatever happens to us, we center our minds and thinking on Jesus who gave Himself for us. That's the message of Lent. We center our thinking on the cross and on Jesus in the time of Lent.

Jesus Is King and Our Friend　　　　2 Lent (C)

Object: Symbol: - IHC (Jesus)　　　　　**Luke 13:31-35**

This strange symbol for Lent has three letters. Let us start with the background color. What color is it? Purple. Purple is a main color in Lent. Purple represents beauty. What else? Royalty! Like in government and power! In church you will see that the pastor might wear something with purple. Or the altar furnishings have purple colors. Purple is also the color that reminds us of forgiveness. Purple is the main color for Lent.

Let us look at the strange letters. This is a very interesting symbol for Lent. It looks like an "I" and an "H" and a "C". These three Greek letters spell out as a symbol the name of Jesus in Greek. So the "I" is like J, and the "H" is like an S, and the "C" is another S. The word is JeSuS.

Symbols help us worship. These letters are symbols that give us a message. The message of the symbol is that Jesus is king and Lord. The IHC stands for the name of Jesus, and the purple color points to Jesus as the royal king.

In Lent, we honor Jesus as king. When Jesus came into the capitol city of Jerusalem, He knew He loved the city. He knew He would be willing to die for all the people there and for us who believe as well. He is our friend. We are friends with a king. A great friend is willing to die for a friend. A friend is a person we trust and can depend on. We all need friends, at least one good friend for sure. Friends are not easily made. Most people have to work on being friends with someone. I know you have a friend. His name is Jesus. Jesus is our friend and king. We can trust Him to rule our lives so we can do God's will and receive the Lord's blessing. Children, live your life for the Lord.

Lesson:
Bear Fruit

Object: Figs/package of   Luke 13:1-9

For our Gospel reading and object lesson, I have a couple of figs. Figs are not a vegetable, they are a fruit. Figs grow on trees. Trees are good because they give some wonderful fruit. What are some fruit that come from trees? Apples, oranges, pears, plums, bananas. And now, figs. Mothers can make wonderful pies from fruit, like peach pie and apple pie. But, whoever heard of fig pie? No one! Me, either!

In Jesus' country, all the people loved figs. I'll bet they had fig pie, too. Those people liked to watch the fig tree grow. Slowly. All trees have blossoms. The blossoms are the beginning of the fruit. But there are no blossoms on a fig tree. The pollination came from one, and only one, little insect—a fig wasp that bores a hole from hole to hole. The little insect must do its work of going from tree to tree, branch to branch and bud to bud.

Have you every watched a honeybee go from flower to flower? As it collects syrup for honey, it also pollinates. The same is true with the fig tree. Sometimes there was a problem. If there was no insect, there would be no fruit, then the tree was good for shade only. A fig tree is poor shade. So if there were no figs and poor shade, that tree was in trouble.

Jesus told a story that our lives were a lot like a fig tree. God made us to do good things with our life, things that make Him happy and other people happy, too. When there are many figs, everybody is happy. When you do good, your mother is happy. Your dad is happy. Your family is happy. Do not stop being a good fig tree. We need others to help us, to care for us. Bear fruit and do good, because you are loved, just like a good fig tree.

Lesson:
Feel You Belong

Object: Cup, Personal/Coffee or silver   Luke 15:1-3, 11-32

The Gospel reading is the story of two brothers, a younger brother and an older brother. The older brother stayed at home. The younger brother got some money from his father and went away from home. He thought everything was going to be so nice and so great, but it wasn't. What he didn't remember was that his mother and especially his father were at home, worrying and waiting.

When the young son did come home, broke and hungry, the father got the best calf for a feast of roast beef and they had a big celebration. He told his servants to get a nice robe and a coat, and to put a ring on his finger, a new pair of shoes on his feet. Also waiting for him at home would be a hot drink in a nice cup.

Maybe it was something like this cup. Now, this happens to be my very personal coffee cup. This is the only one in my house like this. I like this cup. There's none other like it. It is a special cup given to me by special people for a very special occasion.

In a Jewish home every boy had a special personal cup. When that boy came home, his father had that cup waiting for him. Do you know what that cup told that boy? It told him that he still belonged in that family.

We all need to belong. What in your family tells you that you belong? Do you have a special chair to sit in? Your bed? Your room? What tells you that you are wanted? Do you have your own cup to drink from at home? That tells that you belong.

Belonging is very important in our lives. When we feel we do not belong to anyone, we are sad. Belonging give us security. Belonging in your family is extremely important, and that's a very, very wonderful feeling to have.

Lesson:
Live for Jesus
5 Lent (C)

Object: Stone - Direction/Corner
Luke 20:9-19

In our Gospel reading, Jesus told a story about some farmers. The farmers are like us. They have been given things to do. They have purpose and goals. These farmers had a grape farm—called a vineyard. The owner sent for some grapes. The farmer didn't want anyone to come and tell him and his servants what to do, so they beat up on everybody. Several people were sent. The same thing happened to each of them. Finally, the owner sent his son. The son was killed. That was a terrible thing to do.

The people did not like this story very well as it seemed rather strange. They knew Jesus was a great storyteller. Usually the stories were about the things people could see, and they always had a great meaning. Most of the time they had to do with what they believed about God. Sometimes the stories were about them. This time they did not know what it meant. When they asked, Jesus told still another story which they didn't seem to understand either.

First Jesus told of the son of the owner who was killed. Then Jesus went on to tell about a cornerstone which gave a correct direction for construction. They were confused and getting suspicious. Jesus said, "It is like a stone that a builder needs to make a building straight. You need a direction stone. You need to know the place to begin to build if you want the best."

What Jesus meant was: If the son is killed as he is in the story, and if the best stone is thrown away, then you will never get God's goodness and best.

This stone is like Jesus. He gives our life direction. Everybody has bad days. Life is up and down. The stone that the builders rejected was the best stone. They did not know that, but we do. The son was God's son.

Lesson:
Jesus Is My King   Passion Sunday (C)

Object: Word: King and Palm Branches   Luke 19:28-39

In the Gospel reading, the people shouted, "Hosanna to the King!" The word Hosanna is Hebrew meaning "Save, we pray." Kings can save people. We call this Sunday both Palm Sunday and Passion Sunday. It's the Sunday that has to do with Jesus as the king. It's exciting to be a king, but it's not very easy. It would have been easy for Jesus to have been on the sidelines. It would have been safe to be there instead of riding on the donkey into Jerusalem. But God had special work for Him to do as the king. So He was obedient. He went into Jerusalem to become the king.

What this Sunday means is that Jesus comes to us as the king. That's really very exciting. He wants to be our king as well and wants to rule in our lives. That means He is our master. Whatever He wants us to do, we do it because He is our king and we love him. A king is one who rules, who controls, who says you do this and we gladly do it.

We have the palm branches because this is a very significant Sunday. We have waved them around to remind us that Jesus is our king. People waved palm branches in the olden days, just the way we would wave a big flag to honor someone. We honor his rule. What does a king do? He loves you and he takes care of you. He provides for our needs. Makes us safe. Helps us to do our best. Wears beautiful clothes. We have a beautiful purple color in the season of Lent to remind us of the royalty of the king. Jesus is our king. He gives us the things we need because he loves us. I want you to say with me, "He is king."

Lesson:

Jesus Is Risen

Easter Sunday (C)

Object: Easter Lily

Luke 24:1-11

ook at all the Easter lilies our families have provided for our church. We want to talk about this lovely, stately lily. There are more than two hundred different kinds of this flower. Notice that the lily stands up straight and tall, like it has a message to bring to everyone who looks at it. We call this flower an Easter lily because it has been cultivated and grown just for this wonderful celebration.

Notice the beautiful green color of the plant. Green is the color we usually associate with growth. We think of trees that grow leaves and green flowers and the green grass. We know green means growth. So the green on this plant tells us something about new life, doesn't it? It is green and alive.

The petals are like a horn. The petals are colored white. Inside are the pistil and stamen, which are yellow. On the bottom is the sepal. Flowers have four main parts.

Today we're celebrating because Jesus has risen from death into new life. Easter is exciting because new life and hope come through resurrection. Easter Sunday is very special for all of God's people. We are all dressed in our very best. We worship on Easter Sunday because Christ has risen.

I want you to say that with me. "Christ has risen."

Once more. "Christ has risen."

That's what these flowers are saying as these white horns point in different directions. They are proclaiming to everybody that Christ has risen. The beautiful white color tells us that there is purity. We praise the Lord for the power of the resurrection. All the beautiful Easter lilies give us the lovely fragrance of the resurrection.

Lesson:
Believe What You Cannot See

Object: Wind

On this Sunday after Easter I have someone with me that you cannot really see nor touch. I will give you some hints to help, and you guess. I brought it with me, but it usually lives outside. We know he is around, because he usually stirs things up and often gets into trouble. Just when we have the leaves raked into a pile, he comes and messes it up. When the windows are open, he moves the curtains. He rattles doors. He pushes snow into big drifts. Who is our nearly invisible friend? The wind!

When Jesus rose from the tomb, He came to visit the disciples and some followers. All were present except Thomas. Thomas heard the story that Jesus had been raised from dead and had been there to visit, but he didn't believe it. He said, "Unless I can see, I will not believe. I must touch him." Thomas wanted firsthand information. He wanted the experience for himself. "Give me facts," was his request.

A week later, the disciples were together again, and Thomas, too. The risen Lord Jesus came softly into their midst, like a breeze. He came from nowhere, like the wind. Jesus said, "Put your finger here in my side. Touch me, Thomas." Thomas said, "My Lord and my God." Thomas doubted no longer. He believed. Then Jesus said to all of them, "Do you believe because you see me? Happy are those who believe without seeing me!" And Jesus was gone, just like the wind. We know Jesus is alive and present with us, too, just like the wind. He is present, invisible and powerful. When you feel the wind—soft, gentle and warm—remember this story of Thomas and the risen Lord. God bless you all.

Lesson:

Listen and Do

Object: Fishing Net

Our Gospel reading and this fishing net are like a bat is to a ball. Here is the story. When Jesus was put on the cross, the disciples did not know how to help, so they went home. Some of them went back to the place by the lake where they lived, called the Sea of Galilee. The very night they got home, the disciples went back to fishing which was a good occupation. They fished all night in the moonlight. They put their nets out on the right side of the boat, then on the other side. They put their nets everywhere and they did not catch a thing. Nothing!

A man stood on the shore watching them cast their nets. He looked like a regular man to them, but the man was the resurrected Jesus.

He said to them, "Take your net and put it over on the right side and you will get some fish." They thought to themselves, "No way, we've had our nets on all sides of this boat all night long and we've caught nothing." But they listened to Jesus, and they caught a big mess of fish.

This story in the Gospel is very difficult to describe. Many things can be said about it. But one thing for sure, the disciples did what Jesus asked them to do. They listened. How many of you think it's important to listen? Your moms and dads will be proud of you. All of you believe it's important to listen. And to DO what Jesus asked you to do.

Do you know what? The disciples caught so many fish they thought their net was going to break. When we fish, it is good to listen to and to watch those people who are already fishing. Chances are, they are there for a reason: good fishing. It is important to listen to what Jesus wants us to be and to do.

Lesson:
Listen to Jesus   4 Easter (C)

Object: Flute/shepherd's or band instrument   John 10:22-30

I am holding a flute. This is a genuine shepherd's flute. I actually bought it from a shepherd just outside the city of Bethlehem. I listened to him play it. It had a lovely, haunting sound, like a flute far off in the night. Everybody likes music. People of every nation have music, each in their custom. Many people have some kind of an instrument like it.

Shepherds use a flute when they are out in the fields with their flocks. At night, the sheep will be quiet as the shepherds play. They will not be restless and stray away. Sheep seem to know the music from their shepherd.

We know that sheep recognize the voice of the shepherd. They will follow the voice. They will gather around the shepherd. There were people who questioned Jesus about His teaching. They wanted to know if Jesus was really from God. Jesus said to them, "I told you once, and you would not believe. You are like sheep who do not belong in my flock."

Jesus as the good shepherd wants us to follow His voice. He wants us to listen to His voice. How does He speak to us? One way is through the Bible. Even if you are very young, you will want to study the Bible because that is one of the ways Jesus comes to us. We want to hear the voice of Jesus speak to us.

Jesus also speaks to us in prayer. We must listen, as well as talk, in our prayer. It is just like listening to a flute. You have to stop talking and listen. When someone sings, we stop talking, tune our ears and hear the words. So also with Jesus. We follow His voice, just the way He told the disciples. "My sheep hear my voice…and follow me." Listen to Jesus, and follow Him. He is the good shepherd.

Lesson:

Heal Hurts

5 Easter (C)

Object: Band-Aid

John 13:31-35

Who of you has been hurt recently? What happened? Squeezed a finger? Stubbed your toe? Got a bump on your head? Fell down really hard? Everyone gets hurt sometime. Pain tells us we hurt.

I have a little package. We open it up, and on the inside is what? A Band-Aid! These bandages are very important to us all. We use them for cuts, for scratches, for ouches. We need lots of love, lots of comfort and healing.

Jesus said to the disciples, "I am giving you a new commandment: Love one another. As I have loved you, so you must love each other." He said to His disciples, "By this everybody will know that you are my disciples, if you keep on showing love for one another." Jesus healed many hurts with His love.

The best way to heal a hurt is to surround it with love. Love is a wonderful salve. It is great medicine. Sometimes we don't have a big hurt on the outside. Where is the hurt? On the inside. It is hurt feelings. How can you put on a Band-Aid when your feelings are hurt? You need more than just a Band-Aid. You need what Jesus meant in the new commandment of love. Comfort, care and concern! Hurt feelings need hugs, time to be held and whispers of love. When those kinds of hurts come, we need mothers and fathers to use the Band-Aid on the outside, and love with hugs to heal the inside.

Life is like that sometimes, there are hurts. We need Band-Aids and love. Love heals hurts. Learn to heal hurts with love. Band-Aids are good and necessary. Love, with hugs of care and comfort, is free and surely important. Learn to heal hurts outside and inside. The next time you have an ouch, put on a Band-Aid, and remember Jesus' word: Love one another.

Lesson:
Sometimes We Are Afraid 6 Easter (C)

Object: Blanket - security John 14:23-29

I have in my lap a nice, soft, warm blanket. What is it called? A comfort blanket. But if I put my thumb in my mouth like I was upset and afraid, then what would it be? Yes! A security blanket. Maybe it is called "my blankie." We need comfort from fear and hurt. The blanket makes me feel safe. How many of you have a little blanket like this? Some children's comfort blankets are all worn out. They are in shreds. But they still give comfort and a safe feeling.

In the Gospel story for today, Jesus was telling the disciples about love. He constantly reminded them of love as a way to make God happy. "Love the Lord your God with heart and mind and spirit" was a very old commandment. The disciples knew about such love.

Jesus said the Comforter would also remind them. He also said He would leave them. They were upset and afraid that Jesus would even suggest leaving them. It did not seem fair. It was not right. They wanted Jesus to be king—not to leave them. The disciples wanted peace. Jesus said he would give them peace. Yet, they were afraid. Jesus said, "Be not afraid." But they were afraid.

We know from other stories in the Bible that fear was everywhere. Fear is common to all of us. Fear is as necessary for life as is pain. Pain is necessary so that we know we are in danger. If you are too close to a stove burner, you sense danger. If you squeeze your finger in the door, you sense pain and get help. So, fear is good sometimes. When danger is near, we are alert. We look. We listen. We sense. We hear. Pain and fear are built into us for safety reasons. When we are afraid, or in pain, we remember Jesus, His love and promise. He brings us comfort and strength. Blankets are good!

Lesson:

We Are One in Christ

Object: Cross/wood or paper sign painted/altar or pectoral John 17:20-26

Jesus wants all of us to be able to pray, and to believe in the power of prayer. We are to pray always, in the name of Jesus. Jesus taught the disciples and others how to pray. He gave an example of prayer, which we call the Lord's Prayer. We pray His teaching prayer very often. Some people call that prayer the "Our Father," or "The Lord's Prayer." Jesus prayed for Himself often. You would expect that He prayed! He found time to pray alone.

In our Gospel story, the reading is about Jesus' personal prayer. We call it the "high priestly prayer." In it He prays for Himself and the Father. But Jesus prays for the whole world. His prayer is that everyone who believes His word should be one in spirit.

Our faith in God our Father and the Lord Jesus, by His grace, make us one in spirit and fellowship. Of course, we are very different in most things. But in Christ, we are one. I am wondering how we can understand that we are all one in Christ. I have this idea.

Everyone stand up. Let us stand close together and form a big circle that looks like an "O." Our circle will stand for the letter "O" meaning one. What do we need to make us the family of God? How do we know we are the community of faith? How will all of us know we are one as Christians? That we belong to Jesus?

The answer? We will put this cross right into the center of our circle. All Christian people recognize the meaning of the cross. The cross tells us that our Lord Jesus Christ took the sins of all who believe, and forgave them. So where shall we put the cross? In the middle of our "O" circle, in the center of our lives. Right there in the middle. Everybody say: "We are one! In Christ!"

God Wants Us to Witness Pentecost Sunday (C)

Object: Bird/Dove/picture of or sculpture John 15:26-27, 16:4-11

I have a picture of a bird. What kind of a bird is it? A dove. When Jesus was baptized, a dove flew near and a voice said, "You are my son." The dove is a symbol of the Holy Spirit. The Holy Spirit empowered Jesus for ministry. After His baptism, Jesus preached the good news. He healed and comforted people. He challenged those who would not believe.

Today is a Sunday called Pentecost. We celebrate this Sunday as the beginning, the birthday of the church. When you were (or are) baptized, you were "indwelled" with the Holy Spirit. The Holy Spirit in your heart and mind was God's gift to you. That makes you a member of the body of Christ.

You have power as a Christian to be in unselfish prayer. You have power to witness of Jesus' love and forgiveness. We are empowered with gifts and fruits of the Spirit to be strong in the Lord. There are many places in the Bible that tell about these gifts. Some of the gifts are hope, faith and love.

In the Gospel reading today, Jesus promised the disciples that they would receive a special gift from God called the Counselor. He is very powerful. He is good. He is strong. He will help us witness. The dove is God's witness to us.

At the end of our story today is a question. How do we witness to each other? I will help you: By being here together. By talking about Jesus' love. By singing and praying. By telling someone who does not know of Jesus, that Jesus loves them.

You can say to a friend, "You see this bird? It is a sign of the Holy Spirit and of Jesus." It reminds me that God wants us to do one very important work for Him. Witness. That's the key word. God wants us to witness of His love!

Lesson:

God Is One in Three

Object: Circles; Three/intertwined, as a triangle   John 16:12-15

Sometimes we call God "Our Father." But God is also Jesus who is God's Son. And we have the Holy Spirit. All three—Father, Son and Holy Spirit—are God. But there is one God, and only One.

There are many people who wonder about our God. How can God be one and at the same time be three? That is a mystery, which we will never be able to describe. The Bible does say God is one.

Jesus said that the Father and Son were one. How can two be one?

If we add the Holy Spirit, we have how many? Three! Father, Son and Holy Spirit. Jesus said that when the Spirit of truth comes, He will guide us into all the truth. We need to hear those words. The Bible does not use the word Trinity. The church made up that word to help us understand God.

So children, how shall we picture this lesson? There is one God, who is also three, as the Bible tells us. I have these three circles. One is hooked to the other two so that they are intertwined. It looks like a triangle of circles.

The circle stands for the eternal. God will never go away. He was from the beginning. He is now. He will be forever. The Father, Son and Holy Spirit are always with us. Yes, see how they interlock. They are never alone. They are three in one. And look, the circles are equal. They form a triangle!

When we pray, we pray in the name of the Lord Jesus. We pray also "Our Father." We ask for the power of the Holy Spirit. So we have a special Sunday called Trinity Sunday. It comes only once a year. It is always the Sunday after Pentecost. When you see circles, think about God as Father, Son and Holy Spirit, and be reminded that our living God is Three in One.

The stories that are told in this section tend to be generic because they relate to a special day or subject rather than a text or an object. There are special days of the church year and national holidays, which are recognized in the church. Lessons for children are always appropriate during these special days.

There are many ways to tell a story. Some storytellers prefer to walk as they talk. I suggest you sit with the children gathered around you. If you are in a church setting, sit facing the audience, with the children facing you, their backs to the people. You will have better control and eye contact with the children.

When the children understand the point of the story and lesson, so will the adults. Try not to speak to the adults of the congregation through the children and your story. You will get trapped every time, because the adults will know you violated the story and spoke to them rather than the children.

Of course, you can read the story as I have written it, but it will be so much better if you can memorize the ideas and share them as your story.

Always have the object available. Be creative. Have fun. The children will love your storytelling and so will the congregation. Always be ready for a surprise from the children. You never know how one of them will respond. Some times families' secrets get leaked out. When that happens, just go right on with your story. Don't be tempted to pick up on the surprise the child might have shared. It might be embarrassing in the sense that the child might have overheard a family secret or perhaps had been entrusted with it.

Of course, you are free to use these stories in any way possible to help you teach a lesson in church, in school and home. Enjoy and give thanks to the Lord for His special blessing to each of us.

Lesson:
We Prepare for the
Coming of Jesus in Advent

Object: Advent Calendar

Luke 1: 26-38

*A*n Advent calendar has windows or doors you open up, one for each of the four Sundays. Underneath is a picture and a verse of Scripture. Look carefully! Do you see that each picture is numbered, from one and up. That means you can open one each day of Advent. Each picture will have a little picture and story about Advent, what it means and what we are expecting. Advent means "coming," that we are expecting something to happen.

Let's open the window for number one. What does it look like? A man is preaching saying, "Prepare the way." That would be John the Baptist. He is one of the great people who prepared the way for Jesus to come.

Let's look at one more. You pick a door. Okay, that's the ninth! You open it and see what's there. What does this look like? Looks like Mary and an angel. The angel is saying to Mary that she is going to have a little baby. Will the baby be a boy or a girl? The angel said it would be a boy. We know what that baby's name will be, don't we? The baby will have the name Jesus.

Let's go to another one. How about that one? Open it. What's that picture? It looks like someone with Joseph and Mary. Where do you think they might be going? To Bethlehem. That's right. Might they be going on a picnic? Well, Mary and Joseph might have had a picnic along the road.

Maybe you could ask your mom and dad to get an Advent calendar at one of the Christian supply stores or at a bookstore so you can have your own. That way, you can prepare for the coming of Jesus. Are you already waiting for Christmas? Wonderful is the birth of Jesus!

Lesson:
Meaning of Christmas

Christmas Eve

Object: JOY – Word

Matthew 1: 18-25

We are celebrating the birth of Jesus, who is our Lord and Savior. The Bible said Jesus came to be our Savior. That was the message of the angel who came to the shepherds out in the fields watching over the sheep. Then a large group of angels joined into a chorus and they sang a beautiful song about the birth of a baby to be called Jesus. We have called this Christmas.

Tonight (or today) we are all happy. We rejoice. We are filled with joy. Have a look at this sign. JOY is a great word in the church. One of our favorite Christmas songs is "Joy to the World". Jesus brings us joy. We want joy. Let me tell you how to best get joy and keep it. Be in the third place, not always first nor second, but rather third, that's how!

J = Jesus. He is first.
O = Others. They are before me.
Y = You. You (and I) are third.

That's the secret. Put Jesus and others first. When you put Jesus first in your life, you have the correct order, the right way to think about what you want and do. If you get a favorite toy and someone else wants it, it would be hard to give it up. However, your unselfishness and your willingness to make someone else happy would be what Jesus wants. So, you do it. You give away your favorite toy (with your parents' permission, of course). You put others first. Jesus and others, then you. Now all of you know the way to have joy. Put yourself last. Then you will become first!

You say with me, "I want to have JOY this Christmas!"

Blessed Christmas to all of you!

104

Lesson:
Jesus Is Our King

Object: Star (Silver or Foil)

Matthew 2:1-12

I have a star. I want to tell you a story with this star, about the wise men who wanted to find baby Jesus. They came from many miles away. They were rich and very powerful. They followed the star, which took them to Jerusalem, the capitol city. When they asked for "the baby born to be king," the answer was—He was born in Bethlehem. That village was about six miles south of Jerusalem. They were very close, so the wise men went there.

When they arrived in Bethlehem, Jesus was not just a baby. He was several months old. They found baby Jesus and presented very costly gifts: frankincense, myrrh and gold. We all know that gold is a precious metal. Frankincense is a resin used to make a powder. It gives off a sweet aroma. Myrrh is a sap from a tree. From it comes a sweet, fragrant perfume.

We call the day on which the wise men came Epiphany. It means that Jesus was revealed as the Savior and Lord of all people everywhere who will receive Him as king. They looked for a king and they found Him. We can say, "Wise men find Jesus and follow Him." That is a smart answer!

Jesus is our king, too, and we want the meaning of Epiphany to be in our lives. We want to follow the star and let Jesus be our king. He came to rule in our lives in everything that we are and do. He is our Savior.

Please say with me, "I want Jesus to be the king and ruler of my life."

Say it with me again, "I want Jesus to be the king and ruler of my life."

In the song, "Silent Night" the last line says, "Jesus, Lord, at Thy birth." That's what Epiphany is all about! Jesus is Lord at His birth.

Lesson:
Introduce Lent

Object: Purple Colored Cloth   Matthew 6:1-6, 16-21

Lent is a time in the spring, a season of forty days plus the six Sundays before Easter. To help us understand what the season of Lent means, I want to show you a very lovely and beautiful piece of cloth. What is the color? Not blue and not lavender, but purple. Isn't this a beautiful color? Why do people wear purple? For importance! Of course! That is correct.

Purple is the color of the altar covering and the pastor's stole. This color symbolizes our sorrow and repentance. Repentance is to tell the Lord we are sorry for our bad behavior and for nasty words in our talk. We want the Lord's forgiveness for anything we have done wrong.

Lent is a time set apart to do something special for yourself and for others in the name of the Lord. It is a time for special study, for prayer and for worship. It is a time to remember Jesus and to give ourselves again to Him. Lent is not so much a food or thing that we give up and will not do. Lent is more of something good that we will do for ourselves and for others in the name of Jesus.

Every time you see purple, remember Jesus. Remember that you love Him, and He loves you very much. Purple reminds you of sin and of forgiveness. Purple reminds you that God has loved you an awe-full lot. Purple is a royal color worn by kings and queens. God treats us royally. Purple is a grand color.

In Lent we understand again how much God has loved us, as the Bible verse that says, "God so loved the world that He gave His only son, that whoever believes in Him shall never perish, but have everlasting life" (John 3:16). Where the verse says "world," we can insert our own name. Then we really understand how much we are loved. God gave His son just for you, and for me!

Lesson:
What Our Lord Did for Us
Holy Thursday (Maundy)

Object: Chi Rho, sign or letters

Mark 14: 12-26;
Luke 22: 7-20;
John 13:1-17, 34

On Holy Thursday we think of what our Lord did for us, and we remember who we are as individuals as well. It is a day for reflection and looking inside.

I have a symbol with two letters of the Greek alphabet. What does this one stand for? The X = Ch in English. (ka hi) Can you say "Kia"?

What is this one? It looks like a P? It is the letter "R" in Greek.

Now, take these two: CH (X) and R (P). Put them together. What does it sound like? Chr(ist).

On Holy Thursday, Jesus gave us the Lord's Supper for the first time. Before that, for many, many years, God's people celebrated with the bread and wine like the Fourth of July and Christmas and Thanksgiving all at once.

What had happened long ago was freedom. The people had been slaves and in bondage. They couldn't do what they wanted. They had to do what the bad kings had said. They wanted freedom and joy and happiness—and they got it. That's what they were celebrating. They ate bread and drank wine to celebrate that day of freedom. Jesus took the bread and wine and gave it to His disciples. But He changed the meaning, saying, "Remember Me, through this meal."

Jesus wants us to remember who He was and what He did as we share the bread and wine. We call this sharing of bread and wine our communion, or the Lord's Supper. Sometimes it is called the Eucharist. That's a fancy word that means "new grace." The Lord Jesus wants us to remember we are forgiven by His grace and to give thanks for it. The people of old knew God's presence was with them. His presence will be with us, too. Remember the symbol, the Chi Rho.

Lesson:
Jesus' Work on the Cross for Us Good Friday

Object: Magnet, and a Cross John 19:17-30

This magnet is something like Jesus' life. I'll show you why. People were drawn to Jesus. Wherever He went, people came to Him. In fact, people flocked around Him. They wanted to hear Him teach and see Him help people.

The cross represents Jesus' work. The magnet represents His person. The cross and the magnet together tell us much about Jesus and His work. But look what can happen. This small coin separates the cross and the magnet. That's like Judas and the thirty pieces of silver, which came between Jesus and Judas.

Sometimes things we do come between the cross and Christ. We let things happen that hinder the work and person of Christ in our lives. We might scheme to get candy, better grades on our papers, even money. Jesus took the cross for us. He did for us what we couldn't do for ourselves. He paid the cost for our sins. He made things right for us.

Who of you has done something wrong, and you knew it? You did a no-no and as soon as you did it, you knew it would bring something bad to you. What was it? And what happened? Nothing! Because you were forgiven. The hurt that should come to us, because of what we have done, has been taken from us by Jesus and forgiven. We are free. We don't have to pay for our wrong. Does that mean we should just do it again and get more forgiveness? No! That would be terribly foolish!

Jesus wants the very best for us in all that we are and do. That's why He loved us so much He would do His work on Good Friday. What great surprise comes after Good Friday? We will know on Sunday, the Day of Resurrection.

Lesson:

Jesus Went Away for a Purpose Ascension Day

Object: Lift Up Our Heads and Faces   Luke 24:44-53, Acts 1:7-11

*A*fter Jesus' resurrection, He appeared to many individuals and groups of people for forty days. Then what happened to Him? The Bible says, "He was taken up to heaven as they watched Him, and a cloud hid Him from their sight."

We raise our arms and open our hands to help us remember Jesus was taken up into the heavens. You can be sure the disciples and followers of Jesus did the same. They raised their arms and opened their hands as He left them. They wanted Him to stay, yet they realized He was going. The Lord God had plans for the resurrected Jesus. He was going home to be with the Father.

When Jesus was with His disciples and those who followed Him, He tried to open their minds to understand that He must go to His Father so the Holy Spirit could come. But they had difficulty in understanding what the promise meant. Jesus wanted them to know that when the fullness of the Holy Spirit would come, the believers—the Followers of the Way—everywhere in the world could know the Lord and receive His blessing.

Jesus said, "It is not for you to know the times or seasons which the Father has fixed by His own authority" (Acts 1:7).

Jesus promised He would send someone to take His place. Who is that? It is the Holy Spirit. The Spirit came in your baptism and continues to come daily as you ask Him to fill you with His presence and power. The Holy Spirit—who is called the Comforter—will come to everyone who believes and receives the Lord. Do you all need comfort? Of course! We all need comfort and care and love. Ascension is an important event for us because it is the beginning of God's plan to bless you with the Holy Spirit.

Lesson:
God Wants Us to Witness   Pentecost Sunday

Object: Piece of Bright Red Cloth   Acts 1: 1-8 and 2: 1-4

Today is a Sunday called Pentecost. Pentecost means fiftieth day, and it is the seventh Sunday after Easter. The color is always red, because it is an exciting event. The piece of bright red cloth will remind us of Pentecost.

When you were (or are) baptized, you were indwelled with the Holy Spirit. The Holy Spirit in your heart and mind was God's gift to you. Your baptism and the gift of the Holy Spirit makes you a member of the body of Christ, which is the church. The beginning of the church is celebrated this Sunday. It is the birthday of the church.

As little children who believe in Jesus, you have power to be strong in your prayer. You have power in very simple ways to witness of Jesus' love and forgiveness. We, as adults especially, are empowered with gifts and fruits of the Spirit to be strong in the Lord. There are many places in the Bible that tell about these gifts. Some of the gifts are faith, hope and love.

In the reading from the book of Acts, the resurrected Jesus promised the disciples and all who believed in Him that they would receive a special gift from God called the Holy Spirit. Sometimes He is called the Counselor. He is very powerful. He is good. He is strong. He will help us witness.

At the end of our story today is a question. How do we witness to each other? I will help you: By being here together. By talking about Jesus' love. By singing and praying. By telling someone who does not know of Jesus that He loves them. You can say to a friend, "When you see a red cloth, be reminded that it is a sign of the Holy Spirit and of Jesus." The red cloth reminds us that God wants us to do an important work for Him. God wants us to witness of His love!

Lesson:
Freedom to Believe

Reformation Sunday

Object: Word, FREE, As An Acrostic

John 8:31-36

*M*any years ago, a German pastor named Martin Luther began a movement called the Reformation to help people study the Bible in their own spoken language and understand that the Lord loves us as forgiven sinners. Luther wanted people to worship the Lord freely and gracefully.

Today, on Reformation Sunday, we remember Martin Luther as a great man of God. And also we remember that Jesus said in our Gospel reading, "You are free when the Son sets you free."

I have a word I want you to think about. The word says FREE. What does it mean? To be unleashed, like a dog running anywhere! To be unfastened, like a fishing boat. The Lord wants us to be free. At liberty!

The word FREE and Reformation have something to do with each other.

What do you think the "F" might refer to? How about FATHER? Or FORGIVEN? Oh, the word FUN! That's good! When we're free, we can have fun.

What word would we use for "R"? How about a big word like RENEW? You think it should be RUN! Yes, we are free to run and have fun.

We've got two "E's." What shall we consider? EXCITING, that's a good word, and so is EASY. Another one might be EQUAL. When we're free as boys and girls of any race or color, we are free and we are equal.

In the Gospel reading, Jesus said, "If you obey my teaching, you are really my disciples; you will know the truth and the truth will set you free…If the Son sets you free, then you will be really free." Jesus wants us to be free to study and learn. He wants each of you to have the right to believe in Jesus as your Lord and Savior. He wants us to be free to run and have fun!

Lesson:
Our Names Are with the Lord   All Saints Day

Object: Telephone Book   Matthew 5:1-12, Revelation 21: 24-27

How many of you know how to use the telephone? How many of you think you could dial the phone and call me? You would need to get the number from your mom or look in the church directory. Okay. Who thinks they could do it?

What about this thick book? What is it called? A telephone book! You can call somebody if you know their name. Do you know my name? If you know my first name and my last name you could look in this book and find my number and you could call me on the telephone. If you would call me this week, we could have a little visit together. Wouldn't that be fun? I'm sure your parents' names are here, too.

The names of our families and my name being in this book is something like the last verse in the second lesson which was read to us. The Bible says our names are in the Lamb's book of the living. That means our names are in God's book in heaven and we are assured that we are His people. When you are His, as baptized children, you are living in the Lord. Your name is written in the Lamb's book of the living. God has a great book, and I don't know if it is anything like this telephone book or not, but our names are there. That's really wonderful.

Even now, since that's true, we can be talking with God, listening to Him speak to us in prayer any time we want. Just like being on the telephone, we can come to God in prayer. That's really good news. It is as if the Lord wants us to call Him up on the telephone of prayer and ask for a blessing, for guidance and all the good things He has promised to those who believe in Him.

Lesson:
Give Thanks and Share

Object: Special Offering Envelope

Luke 12:22-31

In America we have a day called Thanksgiving Day. It is a part of our history as a nation, as the United States of America. There is much for us as a nation for which to give thanks—freedom, liberty, worship, hard work.

The Bible has a lot to say about the giving of thanks. In one place it says, "In everything, give thanks." That is not always easy, but we know it is good and right, so we gather with many other people to give thanks.

One of the ways we give thanks is to give money so it can be shared with others who are poor. Jesus said, "We always have the poor with us" (Mark 14:7).We are encouraged to give thanks through our gifts of money.

Here is an envelope especially printed for Thanksgiving. Using this special envelope is a good way to give a gift. The question for us on this day of Thanksgiving might be who is poor? Who will decide who will get the money we give? The leaders in our church and community know who has the need and where it is. One half of our giving will go to World Hunger. What about the other half? It goes to help agencies here in our community and town. What are some of the agencies? Who knows? The Mission House. The Dental Clinic. The New Hope Center. The Storehouse. The Helping Hands Mission. All of these and many more. It is good to give thanks to the Lord.

In the Gospel reading, Jesus said, "Do not worry about the food you need. Look at the crows. Look at the wild flowers. Don't be all upset."

Why should we worry? The Lord has promised to help us just like the birds and flowers and all of His creation. The Lord takes care of all of His creation and He loves us, too!

Lesson:
Show Your Love to the Person You Love

Valentine's Day

Object: Card, or Valentine, Heart Shaped

John 3: 16

I have an envelope that doesn't have a name on it. What do you think is in it? Might it be a birthday card? You think it looks like a card for Valentine's Day. You guessed right. Let's see what is written on the outside. "You're the picture of a daughter who's loved in every way." Inside it says, "and you're the darling Valentine who gets this wish today. Happy Valentine's Day." It has Xs and Os on the inside. X's and O's stand for I LOVE YOU.

We give valentines to show our love for others. It's a day to share our love with one another in a special way. Who do you think is going to get this valentine? Who should I give this card to? To my daughter.

Every one of us wants to receive valentines? You each want more than one. Our friends want a valentine from us. Moms and dads want valentines. We all want to be loved? We want to receive love and give it. One way to give love is in the form of a valentine.

The heart is a symbol of love. I hope you all have a valentine to show your mother and father, your family and friends that you love them. But if you don't, what can you do? You can make one. Be creative!

Or, you can love family and friends by giving them a big hug and a kiss on the cheek on Valentine's Day and tell them, "I love you very much." That might mean even more than a card. That's what we want to do for Valentine's Day.

God has loved us in a very special way, too. We have Christmas and Easter where we celebrate God's love to us. He proved His love by giving us His Son. The heart is a symbol of God's love for us.

Meaning of Mother's Day

Object: The Word, MOTHER, As An Acrostic

*M*other's Day is a very special day for all of us. What's so special about this day? We want to honor our mother and our grandmothers today.

MOTHER, written with one letter underneath the other, is called an acrostic. We're going to fill in a word that goes with M, and a word that might go with O, and one that begins with a T and all the way down to the R.

Who has the first word that can go with M? What can we put up there? My—meaning My Mother or My Mom. That would be a good short easy word.

How about for an O? Others! That's a good word. Mothers are concerned about others.

How about the T? Together. Yes! That's a good word. How about another one for the letter T? Talk. Oh, that's an important one.

What's one good word to honor our mothers when she prepares a nice dinner? What's the word that starts with T? Yes, Thanks.

How about the H? Help. Ah, a very good word. What might be another H word. What are we going to do this day that will be special for mother? Besides thanking, we're going to do what, with an H? Hug. Oh, that's a good one. Give her lots of hugs, for sure. You kids are smart. How about Honor? And where do you live? She makes a nice what? She makes a nice Home for you.

How about an E? Eat! That was just too easy.

What about R? You say, Rest. How about the word Respect?

What's another great word that goes with Eat on Mother's Day? It's an R word. I'll tell you what it is, but don't tell your dad. It's Restaurant.

Wow! This will be a special day for your mother!

Meaning of Father's Day

Object: The Word, FATHER, As An Acrostic   Psalm 112

J ust like Mother's Day, Father's Day is a very special day for all of us. What's so special about this day? We want to honor our father and our grandfathers today.

FATHER written with one letter underneath the other is called an acrostic. We're going to fill in a word that goes with F, and a word that might go with A, and one that begins with a T and all the way down to the R.

What word do you think we should put in for the letter "F?" You think it should be Fun. That's great word. You can have fun with your dad. Oh you want to say, Fair! Yes, fair is a good word, too.

What should we use for the letter A? Ask, that's an interesting word. Ask Dad anything. He has an answer. Remember now, this is Father's Day. You could ask what he would like to do this day, or what he wants from you.

How about the T? Thanks. That is a great word for Dad, isn't it!

Let's try the H. Honest, that's a great word. You say Heal Hurts. That is simply wonderful. Many times we want Dad to bring us care and comfort—heal hurts. When we have hurt feelings, we need a Hug from dad. Right!

Now we have the letter E. Remember when we did the E for mother, we said, Eat out. What should we say for Dad? How about enjoy? We want him to enjoy the day. What else? Easy! Yes, we surely want Dad to have an easy day.

The last letter is R. Rest is a good word. Fathers need rest—meaning, not doing anything. How about Renew? Or Reset?

I am sure you will help your father to have the most relaxed day possible.

Remember, it is his day, so honor him in every way.

Lesson:
Our Freedom

Object: Flag

Psalm 46

E verybody knows this is our flag—the flag of the United States of America. This week we celebrate a special day when we will fly the flag. Why do we celebrate? What does the flag stand for? What does it mean?

It means that we have a big celebration, but why? Well, one of the things the flag symbolizes is our freedom. We have freedoms in our country. One of those freedoms is to worship. We come to this church early in the morning and worship. No one tried to stop you from coming. We can sing. We can worship. If we want to give a big offering, we can. If we don't want to give anything, nobody is going to say that we have to do it.

Now, there are some people that don't want to go to church. That's all right, too. They have the freedom not to worship. And so it works both ways.

So if we want to worship, we can do that. Some people want to sleep in. They are free to get up or to stay in bed and rest. We can choose to pray in our homes. Many people have a prayer, called a Table Grace, before a meal. Here is one that I like.

Our hands we fold, our heads we bow,

For food and drink, we thank you now. Amen

Some families have a "quiet" time set aside for devotions—a time for Bible reading, sharing and prayer. That's good, too. It is an opportunity and freedom to share our faith and our love.

We have the freedom to make the choice for or against, to participate or not to participate. Freedom means liberty and the pursuit of happiness. That's some of what this flag stands for. The Stars and Stripes tell us that we are a free people.

Citizenship Memorial Day

Object: Certificate Of Birth or Passport Psalm 91

Matthew was born in Korea, and adopted. As he grew older, he wanted to be an American citizen. Then came the day. He became a citizen of the United States of America. That means Matthew belongs to us and we belong to him. He belongs to this country, and that is really wonderful.

Citizenship is just like baptism. When we are baptized, we belong to Christ and His church. But there are some differences. When we are born in this country, we automatically become a citizen. When we are baptized, the Lord says, "I claim you as my child and make you a member of the church and you are now a citizen in the church." As members of the church, we have privileges and rights. In the church we can pray and worship. We can enjoy people and study. We give honor and glory to the Lord.

We have responsibilities to the church and also to the nation. We support them. We give offerings, and we pay taxes. We vote. We pray for leaders. We witness for Jesus and we defend our country.

Just as we had the ceremonies at the courthouse, where Matthew took an oath to become a citizen and pledged allegiance to our flag, so also was our celebration in the church.

I have a book for us to see. It says, "I am the American Flag." Guess what we will do with this book? We will place this book in the library, in the children's section, in your honor. On the inside is written, "Given to the Church Library in honor of Matthew Jason Elmhorst when he became a citizen of the United States of America." We are happy that we are citizens of the United States of America, and of the church.

Lesson:
Special People

Object: Box and a Mirror

Matthew 19: 13-15

Tomorrow is the beginning of Vacation Bible School. It will be a great week when children and youth come together to study about Jesus. We will have singing. We'll have lots of fun, with many children coming together. It is a wonderful time for very special people who want to come and learn.

I have this beautiful box with wings of silver. In it are some very special people. Would you like to see who they are? Who is that? Who do you see? (mirror) You are seeing yourself. See! All the special people. You are all special, and we need you and want you to be in Vacation Bible School tomorrow.

Who are all these special people? All of us—from age four on up through grade seven are encouraged to come, and to invite your friends. You can bring anyone who wants to meet new people and make new friends.

Oh, you have a new friend down your street. That would be a good person to invite to come. Oh, it's both a girl and a boy. Yes, you ask them both to come. Maybe their parents want to come, too. We need mothers and dads.

Does Vacation Bible School cost lots of money? Yes, everything costs something. But not very much. The church will help with the expenses.

Special people make Vacation Bible School special. We will study about Jesus and His followers. They were known as disciples and as Christians. A Christian is a person who is baptized and believes that Jesus is Lord and Savior.

People anyplace in the world can be Christian. Not only in America, but people of any color and any country. Children who come to Vacation Bible School are special, because Jesus loves them.

Lesson:
Sunday School Is Important
Sunday School Rally Day

Object: Book, Sunday School Materials   Luke 6: 12-19

Next Sunday is an extra special day for all of you because Sunday school starts. Isn't that great? Sunday school is a lot of fun. I encourage you to really look forward to meeting old friends and to bring new friends that you have made this summer. The teachers are prepared and ready for you.

Here's a sample of a new student's book. It is called *God Speaks Through His Word*. That sounds interesting, doesn't it? We all like to know what God has to say to us, and He speaks to us through His Word. If you were to have this in your class, you would learn a lot.

Here's another one. It says *God's Promised People*. In this book you will learn how God showed His love for His people a long time ago. He continues to show how much He loves us. Every one of you is a part of His promised people.

Here's a third book for older kids. It's called *Witness*. There's a picture of Jesus introducing two people to each other. That's what He wants us to do, witness for Him. So if you have any friends or neighbors who don't go to church, invite them to come to Sunday school with you.

And guess what? I hope that every one of you will come to Sunday school and that you will also come to worship service every Sunday. We want your fathers and mothers to come to Sunday school classes, too. Would you tell them that I said they are invited to come to class as well? Sunday school classes are not just for children. All of us need to come to Sunday school for fun and for learning.

Lesson:
Confirmation Is a Promise

Object: Good News Bible   **Romans 10: 9-17**

On Confirmation Day, each confirmand receives the gift of a Good News Bible to commemorate this day for them. Each person's name is beautifully written right in front with a little greeting from this church. As you continue to grow older, and if your family continues to be members of this church, the time will come when you will also get confirmed and receive a very nice Bible like this.

Let me show you several pages. Here is a very colorful map. Oh look, there are many maps of different places. There are many pictures on the inside. Do you see all the very beautiful pictures? This Bible is filled with modern pictures of the Holy Land—Israel.

Just as the church presents these study Bibles as a gift, so God has loved us and given us the gift of His Son, Jesus Christ, who is our Lord and Savior. As you grow in your life with Jesus, it is good for you and for us to remember that God has loved us in Christ Jesus. When we get a nice Bible such as this, it is our remembrance that God loves us.

The Bible is God's word to us. In it are His promises to us of how He has loved us and how the Lord has blessed our lives. All of His goodness is His gift to us. These Bibles are not given just to collect dust and sit around unused. Would it be a good idea, that when a Bible is so worn out that it is falling apart, you could come and trade for a new one? There is a saying: "A Bible falling apart is usually owned by someone who isn't!" We want to help the confirmands remember the promise they make to the Lord and to themselves, to study and learn about Jesus and their faith in Him.

Lesson:
Teaching the Tithe As Stewardship   Stewardship Sunday

Object: Box: 3 Parts (home made)   Luke 6:38

I have a strange box. On one side is written "My Money," and on the other side are the words, "How I Handle God's Gifts." As you can see, there are three compartments in this box. One section says "Church Offering," the middle one is "Spending," and the other is "Saving."

Let's say we have ten quarters (twenty-five cent pieces). The question for us to think about is this? How would you divide the ten quarters so you had some for "Spending," some for "Savings," and some for "Offering"?

I am going to let several of you do this. You think about how you would divide them fairly. How many will you put in the Offering part? Three! That would be generous. We need a lot of church members like you. How much would you put in Spending? Five! That leaves two for Saving.

How about you? How will you divide the ten coins? Two for Offering, two for Savings, and six for Spending. That's a good reasonable combination.

Even though most of you are very small, at your age is the time to begin thinking about your money. How will you use your money?

Tithe is a Bible word that means ten percent, which means one out of ten.

Tithe works like this. If you have ten pennies, one is given away. If you have a hundred, ten would be given. So when we have ten quarters, and we were giving the tithe, how many should go to church? Yes, one!

Stewardship is a Bible word that means managing money and all the benefits that the Lord gives us. We all have money. God can bless us through our money. However, the Lord does expect us to manage well all that we have.

Commitment

Object: Ring   John 2: 1-12

A boy about five years old came to sit on his daddy's lap. While sitting there he noticed his father's ring. He said to his dad, "Where did you get that ring?" The father replied, "Your mother gave this ring to me when we were married." "Really," said the boy, "I don't think I have seen it before." Looking up at his dad, the boy said, "You know, Dad, I am going to marry Mother when I get big."

"No," said Dad. "You can't do that. She is mine. I am married to her."

The boy was not sure about that. Father said, "This ring means we have made a commitment to each other. We have promised our lives to each other. She is mine, and I am hers. We even signed an agreement that states this promise: That we would love and respect each other. We said we would honor and trust each other. We agreed to worship, and play and share together. Isn't that great? Your mother and father have made a commitment."

A ring is important. It tells a story! You might want to ask your father where he bought your mother's ring. Let him tell you how he shopped for it. Was your mother along to help pick it out? Did it cost a lot of money? Was it a big surprise to your mother? How long have your mother and father been married?

Sometimes there are two rings for marriage. One is given before the wedding and one is given during the wedding. Does your mother have two rings? Why does your father have only one?

What happens to rings when grandmothers die? Who gets the rings? There are many questions that can be asked about weddings and rings. Do they ever wear out? When did people begin to wear rings? Did Jesus ever have one? The prodigal son got one from his dad. (See Luke 15:22.)

Lesson:

Honor Marriage

Marriage Enrichment Day

Object: Red Candle

I Corinthians 13

This candle is in honor of the couples who are at the Marriage Encounter Weekend. Notice the candle is red, which is an exciting color for marriage. When the candle is lighted, the flame is red, too, and hot. That's like a strong marriage.   Look at this beautiful symbol. When we look closely, we see there are three symbols all put together into one. See the Heart of Love? There are two rings, which symbolize wedding rings. The wedding rings are like a mother and a father might have. And then there is the cross.

So we've got three parts in this symbol: the heart of love, the wedding rings and the cross. Each of them has special meaning to the couples at the Encounter Weekend.

The Heart of Love: That's a part of what Marriage Encounter is about. We give our love as a gift. We build trust in each other by our honesty with one another. Couples, who have been on a Marriage Encounter Weekend or an Enrichment Retreat, will love and trust each other more than ever before.

The wedding rings tell us that a man and a woman have said to each other: We are in partnership forever. We are a team. We are intertwined. We are together regardless of what life will bring us; we are one in the Lord.

The cross reminds a married couple that they will usually stay together when they honor Jesus who gave Himself for them. A couple who honor and love Jesus will pray with each other and with their children and families. They will worship together, and sing and praise the Lord for His promises.

That's a beautiful combination for a couple and for a family. Husband and wife, the intertwined rings, a love in their hearts and the cross of Jesus.

Lesson:

Ministry Is Serving

Object: Stole

Matthew 28:18-20

The long colorful piece of cloth that a pastor or priest wears over his or her shoulder is called a stole. I want to tell you what it means to have a stole. What a white coat is to a doctor, or a big white hat is to a chef, a stole is to a pastor.

First of all, a stole is a garment a minister wears to show that he or she is a pastor. It is a symbol or a sign that says they have been set apart to do ministry—telling people about the good news of Jesus, in some kind of a special way. Usually ministry is done in a church. However, being a chaplain in the military or a hospital is also ministry.

Every stole can be different. Usually there is a different color on each stole. Blue would be the color for Advent. What color for Christmas and Epiphany? White! Purple for Lent. Green in the summertime. Red is for celebration. Often there is a cross. We all know what a cross is, don't we?

Stoles can be made of different kinds of cloth. Some are silk and some are cotton and some are made from gunnysack—a cloth made from heavy fiber, like a thin twine or rope. Some of it is made from hemp—a very coarse material.

Stoles give us a message about a person's dedication to Jesus and His church—which is the body of Christ and the communion of saints.

Jesus said, "The Son of Man came not to be served but to serve" (Matthew 20:28). He asks us to do the same in Matthew 28:18-20. We are to go and make disciples—tell the good news of Jesus to everyone in the entire world who wants to hear about the promises of the Lord.

Setting

This book, *Gospel Stories for Pastors, Teachers and Parents,* was originally shared with small children ages one to twelve during the congregation's worship service in a large church setting. However, the stories can be told in a small church setting equally as well. I asked the children to come forward and sit with me as the storyteller so that the worshipers could see me and the children.

The stories were called the Children's Sermon, or the Kid's Time or the Children's Lesson. That's the subtitle: *Three Minute Sermons For Kids' Time.* It seemed best to have the story time after the Gospel was read. The telling of the story was intended to single out the point of the Gospel reading for the day, and to be read or told in about three minutes. If the story is being read in the home or school, gather in a comfortable spot where the children can listen without distraction.

If it is to be told in a church setting, the story should be adapted and told in your own words, but it could be read just as easily. In this setting, the story is told to the children with the worshipers listening in on the storytelling. A temptation would be to speak to the congregation through the story. However, a good rule to follow is to make the point to the children. Good chances are that if the children get the point of the Gospel, the adults will, too.

Each story has a tangible object, a simple visual aid. The object is used to help the children understand the point of the Gospel reading. It is vital that there be a connection between the object and the Gospel and the story being told. Try to make more than an impression or just having the children come forward for fun. The purpose is to help them understand the point of the Gospel for the day.

Arrangement of References

There is no easy way nor any single system to organize these stories. In this book, the Gospel readings are cross-referenced numerically, and the object lessons are referenced by page number. What does that mean? And how can it be used to the benefit of the storyteller? There is a deliberate plan in the book and it is user-friendly.

The plan is based on the historical church year calendar. Pastors who preach on these Gospel readings call that calendar, the pericope. When these Lessons are read for church worship services, they are called the Lectionary. In some churches, where there may be no set lectionary, the story would be based on the main Scripture for the day. Those Bible readings were selected for a purpose and reason. In this book the stories tie together the Scripture readings and an object, the visual aid, to help the storyteller with the point of the Gospel for the children. Most churches follow a church year. For many churches, the church year follows the school year. The visual aids, Scriptures and Lessons work together any time.

Historically, the church year begins with the first Sunday in Advent, which is the last Sunday of November or the first Sunday in December. After the twelve days of Christmas comes Epiphany, which is always January sixth.

Between Epiphany and Lent there are often several Sundays. The beginning of Lent, which is Ash Wednesday, depends on Easter which is a moveable date in most churches. The time is calculated by the position of the moon, since Easter is based on lunar time. Lent comes 40 days before Easter.

Pentecost Sunday is always fifty days after Easter, which means the time between Resurrection Sunday and Pentecost is seven Sundays. All the weeks of summer are called the Sundays after Pentecost. The church year is divided into two major parts: Festive and Pentecost.

Object and the Story

A listing of references between the story and the object has been made for your help. The object, which corresponds with the numerical listing of the Gospel reading, is listed by page number. Such a listing is intended to help you find an object and make the object user-friendly to the storyteller, pastor, priest, teacher or parent.

You may want to adapt the lesson to your church or home or setting as is necessary. We hope you will! This book is intended as a resource and springboard for you.

Most of the objects are things which can be found in any house. Others can be located in a church setting. Some can be made. Be creative yourself. Add to and adapt the story to make it personal to the children. If the children understand, so will the adults who listen in on your lesson.

Remember that in any worship setting, you will usually have no more than three minutes for the story time. Get to the *one* point. Share the Gospel. If you are in a home setting, you may want to conclude with a prayer. If you can provide a take-back-to-your-seat piece of art work, that is even better. But make sure it relates to the Gospel and your object.

Always be positive. When something is said or revealed by a child that is funny or innocently spoken, have fun! Take the children's chatter for what it is: innocent words of excitement and enthusiasm. The parents will usually understand. What can you do? You really have no way to anticipate what a child is thinking or what they might say. So just enjoy your time with them and whoever is listening to you. The children will!

The Gospel Texts

The Gospel for reading and preaching in the church calendar year is classified numerically, beginning with the chapter and verse. Such a listing is intended to make the selections user-friendly. The listing for these texts is placed in the back of the book.

Down through the centuries in the historical churches, there have been many such lectionaries called the texts or the pericope. Following the church year, beginning with Advent—the last Sunday of November or the first Sunday in December—the Gospel readings have proclaimed the life of Christ.

In most of the historical churches, such as Roman Catholic, Episcopal, Methodist, Presbyterian and Moravian, there are common sets of texts for preaching and teaching. In the *Lutheran Book of Worship* these texts are called the A. B. C. Series. For the year 2006, beginning with the first Sunday of Advent, which is December 4, 2005, the lectionary will be from the "B" Series.

All the texts for this Festival part of the church year are cross-referenced between the Book of the Gospel—Matthew, Mark, Luke and John—with the chapter and the verse, and the object for easy use. They are listed at the back of the book.

Listing of the Objects

Objects for Holidays and Special Sundays

Listing of the Gospel Lectionary

MATTHEW

1:18-25	4 Advent	A
2:1-12	Epiphany Day	A, B, C
2:13-15, 19-23	1 Christmas	A
3:1-12	2 Advent	A
3:13-17	Epiphany/Baptism	A
4:1-11	1 Lent	A
4:12-23	3 Epiphany	A
5:1-12	4 Epiphany	A
5:13-20	5 Epiphany	A
5:20-37	6 Epiphany	A
5:38-48	7 Epiphany	A
6:1-6, 16-21	Ash Wednesday	A, B, C
6:24-34	8 Epiphany	A
11:2-11	3 Advent	A
17:1-9	Transfiguration	A
20:17-28	4 Lent	A
24:37-44	1 Advent	A
25:31-46	Christ the King	A
27:11-54	Passion/Palm	A
28:16-20	Trinity	A

MARK

1:1-8	2 Advent	B
1:4-11	Epiphany/Baptism	B
1:12-15	1 Lent	B
1:14-20	3 Epiphany	B
1:21-28	4 Epiphany	B
1:29-39	5 Epiphany	B
1:40-45	6 Epiphany	B
2:1-12	7 Epiphany	B
2:18-22	8 Epiphany	B
8:31-38	2 Lent	B
9:2-9	Transfiguration	B
13:33-37	1 Advent	B
14:12-26	Maundy Thursday	B
15:1-39	Passion/Palm	B
16:1-8	Resurrection	B

LUKE

1:26-38	4 Advent	B
1:39-55	4 Advent	C
2:1-20	Nativity	A, C
2:25-40	1 Christmas	B
2:41-52	1 Christmas	C
3:1-6	2 Advent	C
3:7-18	3 Advent	C
3:15-17, 21-22	Epiphany/Baptism	C
4:1-13	1 Lent	C
4:14-21	3 Epiphany	C
4:21-32	4 Epiphany	C
5:1-11	5 Epiphany	C
6:17-26	6 Epiphany	C
6:27-38	7 Epiphany	C
6:39-49	8 Epiphany	C
9:28-36	Transfiguration	C
12:22-31	Thanksgiving Day	C
13:1-9	3 Lent	C
13:31-35	2 Lent	C
15:1-3, 11-32	4 Lent	C
20:9-19	5 Lent	C
21:25-36	1 Advent	C
22:7-20	Maundy Thursday	C
23:1-49	Passion/Palm	C
23:35-43	Christ the King	C
24:1-11	Resurrection	C
24:13-35	3 Easter	A
24:36-49	3 Easter	B
24:44-53	Ascension	A, B, C

(See: Acts 1:1-11 for an Ascension text)

JOHN

1:1-14	Nativity	B
1:1-18	2 Christmas	A, B, C
1:6-8, 19-28	3 Advent	B
1:29-41	2 Epiphany	A
1:43-51	2 Epiphany	B
2:1-11	2 Epiphany	C
2:13-22	3 Lent	B
3:1-17	Trinity	B
3:14-21	4 Lent	B
4:5-30, 39-42	2 Lent	A
7:37-39	Pentecost Day	B
8:31-36	Reformation Day	A, B, C
9:1-41	3 Lent	A

JOHN (cont.)

10:1-10	4 Easter	A
10:11-18	4 Easter	B
10:22-30	4 Easter	C
11:1-53	5 Lent	A
12:20-33	5 Lent	B
13:1-17, 34	Maundy Thursday	A
13:31-35	5 Easter	C
14:1-12	5 Easter	A
14:15-21	6 Easter	A
14:23-29	6 Easter	C
15:1-8	5 Easter	B
15:9-17	6 Easter	B
15:26-27; and 16:4b-11	Pentecost Day	C
16:12-15	Trinity	C
17:1-11	7 Easter	A
17:11-19	7 Easter	B
17:20-26	7 Easter	C
18:33-37	Christ the King	B
19:17-30	Good Friday	A, B, C
20:1-18	Resurrection	A
20:19-23	Pentecost Day	A
20:19-31	2 Easter	A, B, C
21:1-14	3 Easter	C

Listing of the Holidays and Special Sundays

Bibliography

Biller, Tom and Martie. *Simple Object Lessons for Children*. Grand Rapids: Baker Book House, 1980.

Children's Sermon Service Plus. Lima: C.S.S. Publishing Company, Bi-monthly. July 1984 through August 1989.

Holy Bible, RSV. Philadelphia: A J. Holman Company, 1962.

Living Bible. Wheaton: Tyndale House Publishers, 1972.

Morentz, Jim and Doris. *Children's Object Lesson Sermons*. Nashville: Abington Press, 1987.

The American Lutheran Church. *Lutheran Book of Worship*. Minneapolis: Augsburg Publishing House, 1978.

Uhl, Harold J. *The Gospel for Children*. Minneapolis: Augsburg Publishing House, 1975.

Weisheit, Eldon. *Worship Talks for Children*. St. Louis: Concordia Publishing House, 1967.

White, William R. *Speaking in Stories*. Minneapolis: Augsburg Publishing House, 1982.

_____. *Stories for Telling*. Minneapolis: Augsburg Publishing House, 1986.

_____. *Stories for the Journey*. Minneapolis: Augsburg Publishing House, 1988.

Gospel Stories
Order Form

Postal orders: Orval K. Moren
10540 Redwood Street, NW
Coon Rapids, MN 55433

Telephone orders: 763-767-0182

E-mail orders: okmoren@comcast.net

Please send *Gospel Stories* to:

Name: _____

Address: _____

City: _____ State: _____

Zip: _____

Telephone: (_____) _____

Book Price: $12.95

Shipping: $3.00 for the first book and $1.00 for each additional book to cover shipping and handling within US, Canada, and Mexico. International orders add $6.00 for the first book and $2.00 for each additional book.

Or order from:
ACW Press
1200 HWY 231 South #273
Ozark, AL 36360

(800) 931-BOOK

or contact your local bookstore